Glen Watson

2-

The Condo Affair

Glen Watson

The Condo Affair

By

Glen Watson

Published by Glen Watson
USA

2015

ISBN-13: 978-1514146217
ISBN-10: 1514146215

Printed by CreateSpace

Printed in the United States of America

Dedicated to my wife Marg, and our wonderful California neighbors Ann, Louie, John, and Noel, who throw great block parties, and unknowingly gave me many ideas for this book.

Unexpected Guest

She quietly undressed to her panties and bra and moved toward the bed. And despite her exhaustion from the flight, managed a devious smile as she unhooked and removed her bra and then allowed her fingers into the waistline of her silky white bikini panties, pulled them down her smooth legs and slipped into bed. As the moon shined through the open blinds, she snuggled against his backside then reached around and put her hand on his stomach and kissed the back of his neck. As she stroked his firm stomach, her smile turned to a puzzled expression and her hand moved lower, reaching another firm object.

"You're not Phillip."

He whispered, "No."

She shook her head, "Oh God, I'm so sorry, so embarrassed. I guess I'll just, well I don't know. I don't know. I'm just so tired."

"It's okay. You don't have to go. We'll straighten it out in the morning. Just go to sleep."

She said, "Are you sure?" He nods, and she whispers, "Oh, thank you." Then she sighs and chuckles a little.

He drowsily asked, "What?"

She shook her head, "Oh, nothing, it's just one of those things that pop into your mind. It's rather crude."

"You have to tell me."

She nods and said, "Well, I was thinking it seems to be quite straight already."

He smiled, shook his head and said, "Just go to sleep."

A mysterious sound of babies crying woke Charlie from a peacefulness of sleep he hadn't had for years, and a perfect dream that hadn't turned in a nightmare, a nightmare of senseless acts for survival, and senseless survival to remember the seemingly senseless acts.

Many times he wished he hadn't survived and figured at some point he would make use of the pistol in the drawer, for he knew that would be his true survival. But this dream seemed to have temporarily replaced the nightmares of the bullet and bomb ridden bodies of friends and foe, neither of which spent their childhood thinking about being involved in the senseless mutilation endeavor. Maybe the dream was a turning point or perhaps merely a break to get him through the night.

The baby crying seemed to be coming from the canyon directly behind his newly purchased condominium. And the crying struck him as quite odd because it seemed to be coming from the old ranch in the canyon where he didn't think anybody lived. Finally the sound faded, and though it was a little earlier than Charlie normally woke up, he felt refreshed from the cool crisp air coming through the open door that led to his lower patio area.

And the girl in the dream, by any means, was not a distraction from his perfect night's sleep. He smiled, for he knew exactly where the dream came from as he recalled the conversation with the realtor who said, "You should get those locks changed on the place right away. That young guy that was staying there, you know the owner's son, well he looked like he probably had a lot of girl friends and may have given the key to some them."

Charlie had replied, "Yeah, That'd be a hell of a problem, a twenty-three year old beautiful young woman attacking me in the middle of the night. You're right, sure helps to have a real estate professional such as yourself."

He then chuckled a little to himself thinking about some twenty-three-year old girl using her key to sneak in and take advantage of a fifty year old. Though still a mystery, he put the baby-crying sound to the back of his mind and the twenty-three year old out of his mind. Then he smiled as he thought about the dream. Sure wouldn't hurt to have that again.

The Condo

Just thirty days ago, a realtor brought him to this condo. He still remembers stepping through the front door into the living room. On the far side of the living room was a large sliding door that opened to a deck on the back of the condo. As he walked across the living room to the sliding door, he was greeted by a spectacular view overlooking a large grass covered canyon with a group of trees in the center. And after getting a closer look at the canyon below, there appeared to be an old farmhouse partially hidden by the trees. Charlie opened the sliding door and walked onto the wooden deck that stood about twelve feet above a slope that gradually extended to the base of the canyon. He made a slow panoramic sweep from East to West and then stopped in amazement, for off to the West he could see a speck of the ocean between branches of the overgrown acacia trees that had sprung up behind all of the condos that overlooked the canyon. No, he couldn't hear the ocean waves crashing against the beach and rocks, or feel the salty spray from heavy surf, but to Charlie, this place had an ocean view, even though it wasn't much. An ocean view and the old ranch below gave him energy that he hadn't felt in a long time. What he didn't know, was that if he could have seen the view through the overgrown trees directly to the North, over the top of the farmhouse, he also would have seen snow on the distant mountains. Imagine having a view of snowy mountains and the ocean with just a slight movement of the head.

As the realtor and Charlie stood on the deck, the realtor said, "You might think this view is nice now, but once those trees are trimmed you'll have a spectacular view."

Charlie nodded, "Yeah, if I had this place that'd probably be my first job, trimming those trees."

"No, you wouldn't have to do a thing. It's a common area. The homeowner's association takes care of all the common areas."

Charlie had never lived anywhere that had a homeowner's association that took care of the yards. He had always taken care of his own yard in the houses that he previously owned, even though most of his neighbors hired gardeners to do it for them. It no longer seemed fashionable for people to do their own manual labor. And it had been years since he'd seen a young person mowing a lawn or doing yard work.

And housewives in the neighborhoods had cleaning women, including the ones that didn't work outside the home. Not that stay at home moms have it easy, for the problem could be that the huge houses in style now were more house than they needed and took more time to clean.

Charlie had the impression at his previous homes, that those who didn't know him, thought he was the only Caucasian gardener in the county. And he was also the only one in his entire neighborhood that washed his own car. He recalled the day his neighbor and the neighbor's young daughter were outside watching Charlie wash his car and the young daughter, with a mystified expression asked, "What's he doing daddy?" The houses were so close together he could hear her question.

The neighbor took a sip of Starbuck's coffee and said, "Oh, he's washing his car honey." Then the neighbor went on to tell Charlie that his time was too valuable to be washing his own car. Of course, as the neighbor was standing there he could have been working with his daughter washing his own car and teaching a lesson that she would have probably enjoyed.

Charlie was thinking that this plumpish, obnoxious, arrogant asshole, who happened to be the worst neighbor that he had ever had, drives five miles to the car wash, waits in a line and drives back home, all of which takes about an hour and a half or two. So obviously, it had nothing to do with time. It was about laziness and trying impress other neighbors, which in his case, wasn't working anyway. Charlie didn't care what the neighbor did or did not do, but he thought the young child was not learning the right lesson, and this could explain why he seldom sees young people doing chores outside.

Even though he previously owned several different houses when he was married, he had never used his military veteran's loan that people referred to as a GI Bill, which was fortunate, because he didn't have the money to put down for a conventional loan. If he obtained an FHA loan, he would have been charged at least fifty dollars a month for private mortgage insurance which they call PMI. The GI bill loan is a good deal for a buyer, but not such a good deal for the seller, because the seller must pay all of the closing costs.

Charlie told the realtor, "I'd like to make an offer, but I'll have to use my GI Bill."

He said, "Okay, I'll write up the offer with GI Bill financing. They may counter and then we can sweeten the deal with a few thousand as necessary."

"No, this will be the only offer that I'll make on this place. It's been on the market for several months." Then Charlie added, "There's a For Sale by Owner two doors down and it's the same model as this one with a similar view."

Shaking his head, the realtor said, "Well, you're taking a chance when you deal directly with a private party. You lose the after sale support that a professional realtor provides and the expertise that is required to complete the complex real estate transaction."

Charlie knew most of complex paper work is taken care of by the escrow company where the details are packaged. However, a realtor has a tough job, for about fifty percent of the people that they transport around looking at property or houses have little or no intention of buying. Some are just lonely, some are just loony, and some just enjoy going for a ride.

Charlie told the realtor, "I've sold a house without a realtor and bought one from a private party and it seemed go quite smoothly."

The realtor said, "Well, things have changed a lot just in the past year. There's a lot more paperwork involved; disclosures, Government requirements; all very complex stuff."

Charlie said, "Seems like the escrow company is the brains of the real estate process. It's kind of like fishing. A child can throw out a lure and catch a fish. But properly cleaning and cooking the fish requires knowledge."

The realtor, getting a little testy, growled, "I'm just trying to keep you from having headaches down the road."

Charlie hoped that the sellers would take his offer, because it was a nice place with two master bedrooms downstairs, each with a full bath, and each bedroom had a sliding door that went out to a lower patio. The upstairs area had a fairly large living room, dining area, and kitchen and a half bath. And it had a two-car garage which really appealed to Charlie because he had a thing for garages.

Charlie's dislike of his realtor started during their first meeting when the realtor told him about the time he was selling his own house, and after the buyer put down a deposit, the buyer decided he didn't want the house. The realtor went through an arbitration to keep the deposit, which might be legal, but most realtors wouldn't have done this. Throughout the buying process, the sleaze just seemed to ooze from this guy like pus from a pimple.

Charlie's realtor called that evening and said, "Congratulations, you just bought yourself a home. The sellers weren't too happy with the offer. And having to pay closing costs didn't thrill them. But, I looked out for you." Charlie didn't know if this was true or not but he was happy with the seller's decision to accept the offer.

At the closing, Charlie and the escrow officer sat at a table in her office with the thick stack of loan documents. Charlie signed and initialed aimlessly wherever she pointed, as they waded through the stack and she explained the few pages that were actually important.

The escrow process has become so muddled with excessive pages of meaningless government imposed bullshit that most buyers just sign everything without reading. Yet, these government rule makers will not take on the title insurance companies that have been overcharging homebuyers far too many years, and the termite inspection industry is starting to push the limit as well.

Charlie was confident that the escrow officer made sure he understood the few important pages, and they completed the process in less than thirty minutes.

Charlie asked, "Does anybody ever read all of this stuff?"

The escrow officer, an attractive and very nice woman, laughed, shook her head and said, "Well, just attorneys, and if the buyers are a married couple, and are both attorneys, they generally argue with each other over each page and it takes several hours."

A week after closing, Charlie's realtor called from an undisclosed location and said, “Congratulations again. Now if you need anything just let me know.”

Charlie asked, “Is the water included in the homeowner fees?”

“I don’t know, but if you need anything let me know.”

The next day he called the realtor and asked him if garbage pickup was included in the association fees.

“I don’t know, but be sure and give me a call if you need anything.”

Charlie was happy there was nothing important that he needed from the realtor and was glad to get the guy out of his life because he had started to be a serious irritant. When he received one of those service rating cards from his realtor, he had to laugh, because he would have had to provide the stamp if he mailed it back.

No Stuff

Charlie wasn't burdened with much of anything. Rather than getting an attorney to battle his ex-wife's attorney, he went ahead and gave her their house and all other possessions, though he did retain his 401K money, but it wasn't accessible unless he wanted to pay the ten percent early withdrawal fee for being under fifty nine and a half.

He drove off in his small pickup with just a few clothes and found it very satisfying and a sense of relief to have nearly nothing. It seemed like a lifted burden and sense of freedom to not have a bunch of stuff. It was as though he had gotten himself buried in nice houses, furniture and things that just kept piling on like a creeping mold that suddenly becomes more suffocating than pleasant. It's almost like an organized hoarding problem that is very cleverly disguised as necessity, elegance, and life style. When something gets a little worn or no longer fashionable you just move it into the garage and replace it with the latest fashion.

Things had been stacking up around him and then he snapped. Well, something snapped. He hadn't figured that out yet. Nor did he think he ever would. He just sort of went nuts. Stuff might have just been a convenient fall guy.

Yet, it's not easy getting by with nothing. Since leaving it all behind, he had bought a small round plastic patio table and four plastic chairs, a small refrigerator, and two queen size beds. The elegant plastic dining set was versatile because it could be used on the deck outside or inside for fine dining. He would have to buy a washer and dryer and maybe a chest of drawers for the bedrooms. But the living room had less than the bare minimum, for it was completely empty. On the convenient side, it was easy to vacuum with no furniture getting in the way.

Canyon View Drive

Wildlife and "wild life" are two different things, and since many of the neighbors were retired and about twenty years older than Charlie, there wasn't much wild life taking place on Canyon View Drive. But a few younger people and a few about Charlie's age or a little younger, made for a good balance. Canyon View Drive was a cul-de-sac with one way in and one way out, so only the residents or guests would have a reason to enter this particular street. But the entire complex, called Ranch Ridge contained 140 units on various streets within the well maintained complex.

Canyon View Drive had a close-knit group of neighbors who held block parties during various times of the year, like fourth of July, Halloween and Christmas.

The neighbors next door to Charlie's condo were the organizers and they even had a roster of names with addresses and phone numbers of most that lived on the street. This closeness of the residents on Canyon View Drive had developed a separation that isolated them from the rest of the large complex. It was as though this street was one large family, whereas the other streets were just individual families that had no block parties or continuity.

Any streets in the complex could have had block parties, but they didn't. Some were satisfied to just be resentful and sometimes hostile to Canyon View Drive residents, and coined the term, "The Canyon People," which they considered a derogatory term, even though the canyon view lots were ten to twenty thousand dollars more than the lots without the view. It just wasn't fair that the Canyon People had a view, parties and fun.

Meeting Lou

A neighbor two doors down, who is about seventy five years old, very distinguished looking, in excellent shape, and looks like he could have been and maybe was in the movies, is picking up the newspaper in his driveway. He waves and walks toward Charlie.

"Good morning. You must be the new owner. I'm Lou."

Charlie smiled and nodded, "Nice to meet you, Lou."

"You've got yourself a good condo complex and a great neighborhood. I think anyway. My wife and I looked at a lot of areas before buying here."

"That's good to hear. I have question for you, Lou."

"What's that?"

"I heard a strange noise this morning, like babies crying. It seemed to come from the canyon below."

Lou chuckles, "Oh, you'll start to like that. They're peacocks. About fifty of them I guess. They live down at the Leo Carrillo Ranch just down below you. You remember the TV show the Cisco Kid. Well, Leo Carrillo played Pancho, the side kick to the Cisco Kid."

Charlie nodded thoughtfully, "Cisco Kid and Peacocks, I'd never have guessed."

"Yeah, I'm a wealth of useless information like that. Look Charlie, I'll get out of your hair. My wife will think I couldn't find my way home. If you need anything like touch up paint or tools, don't hesitate to stop by."

"Thanks, Lou."

Peacocks spend most of their time on the ground feeding on both plants and small animals and are especially fond of snakes and even rattlesnakes. Yet, they are able to fly for short distances to escape attack by coyotes. They warn each other when danger approaches by loud shrieking cries and honks, and that explain the baby-crying sounds. And they also use these sounds during the mating season. They roost in the tree tops at night.

Not only did the peacocks from the ranch provide early morning wakeup calls, the 2500 acre ranch was a haven for numerous wildlife creatures. It was like living in the country with the coyotes howling at night and boldly approaching the condos in search of rabbits, rats, and mice that generally provided their meals. It wasn't uncommon for them to carry off a cat. People who lived on the canyon knew, or soon learned by experience, that an outdoor cat's life span would not be more than a week. A small dog that wasn't on a leash wouldn't last the night and a small dog on a leash had a better chance, but it was recommended that one stay away from the canyon for it wasn't unknown for a coyote to snatch away a small dog despite the leash.

Though Charlie liked dogs and cats, and had no desire that they be carried off by a coyote, he had an admiration for the coyotes. About once a week, in early morning or late evening, he would see one of these beautiful animals with lush fir, as they passed close by his patio in search for food. And each night he could hear them communicating with each other through their eerie howling.

Fox, raccoons, skunks, and rabbits were also abundant and an occasional mountain lion would make an appearance. It wasn't uncommon for rattlesnakes to venture from the canyon into the condo complex and hide in the ground cover along the sidewalks. These rattlesnakes were a hazard that the landscapers encountered and occasionally a dog sniffing during walks would be bitten on the face. Fortunately, most of the bitten dogs survived, by quick thinking owners getting them to a vet.

To Charlie, the most entertaining of all the wildlife were the quail. Even without young ones, their timid and quick movements made them fun to watch. A mother quail, with a brood of chicks to take care of, seemed to operate in a continuous panic mode. Frequently, the skittish mother with a brood of four or five would venture from beneath the brush under the acacia trees and walk past Charlie's lower patio area. During these daring trips, it never failed that a couple of the chicks would slip through the wrought iron fence that enclosed the brick patio of his condo. This made for an interesting scene because the mother quail couldn't fit through the wrought iron bars so she would verbally scold them from outside the cage. Just thinking about the quail would bring a full smile to Charlie's face.

Meeting Fred

Although the view was impressive despite the overgrown acacia trees that were growing on the property behind Charlie's condo, the trees were blocking the sunlight as well as the view, and the branches had extended onto the upper deck. Charlie was standing on his lower patio just outside his master bedroom looking through the branches. He glanced down and saw some black mold starting to form on the exterior stucco near the foundation because it wasn't getting enough sunshine to dry the accumulation of moisture. He started to go inside to get some bleach to pour on the mold when he heard his neighbor's sliding door open and a plump, happy go lucky guy with a round head, saw Charlie and said, "Hello, good morning. You must be the new owner."

Charlie smiled, "Yeah, I'm Charlie Moore."

"I'm Fred. Fred Rice. You know, sort of like fried rice."

"Nice to meet you Fred. I was just looking at the mold that's starting to grow on my foundation."

Fred walked over and looked at Charlie's foundation, and proudly said, "Oh, that's nothing. Come and look at my mold." Charlie walked over to Fred's place and looked at black gunk about a quarter inch thick and extended nearly two feet up the side of Fred's stucco wall. "See what I mean. It's just part of the territory. You know, living on the canyon along with the rats and other critters. Real country like, know what I mean?"

Charlie in a surprised tone, "Rats?"

"Oh yeah, amazing little guys. I've watched them climb up the side of my condo somehow clinging to the stucco. It's just amazing to watch. Get yourself a beer and a chair and it's like watching a trapeze artist at the circus. Those branches that hang over are like a trapeze so they can swing right up on the upper patio and up the side of the condo onto the roof."

"That doesn't bother you?"

Fred looking puzzled, "What do you mean?"

"The rats, they'll get on your upper deck and onto the roof and find a way into your attic."

"Oh, it's just part of the territory. You'll get used to it."

"When will the homeowner's association trim these trees?"

"Oh no, they won't do that. They consider the canyon part of the natural environment. Just like the wildlife."

"Well, I plan to trim the trees so they don't hang over on my patio. And I'd like to get some sunlight back here to keep the moisture down."

Fred shook his head and took on a real serious expression, "You don't want to do that."

Charlie with a puzzled look, "Why?"

"Well, two doors down there was this older couple who were trying to sell their condo because they could no longer do the stairs." Fred hesitates, but continues, "What was their name? Oh, Pat and Tony Apollo. Nice couple, well, a little weird but nice. They stuck to themselves. Anyway, their place wasn't selling because the view was gone."

Fred chuckles, "The view wasn't really gone. It was just hidden from the tall trees. To make a long story short, they hired some of those Mexicans and they took down four trees all the way to the ground. And they had a great view again, just like when these places were new, and within a week the place sold."

Charlie nodded, "Oh, so it's okay to trim them as long as it doesn't cost the association."

Fred gets a very serious expression and starts shaking his head, "Ooh, no. I didn't say that. No, no, no. The trees can't be trimmed. It's an association rule. There's one thing I forgot to tell you. When

Pat and Tony sold their condo the association put a lean against their condo and charged them five hundred dollars for each tree they cut down. Yep, two thousand dollars it cost them."

Charlie did not know anything about homeowner associations, or as most say, HOA, but he would find out as time went by that there seems to be a certain small group who enjoy being involved in that sort of thing. And this works for the majority of condo owners who just turn the decisions over to this small group of people. The HOA is very similar to the government. The majority votes people in and trusts them to do the right things. Hopefully, the system works better in a small organization like the HOA than the government.

The HOA has numerous committees. One is the landscape committee, which is quite popular with women who think they know a lot about landscaping. Generally this committee decides important things, such as the vital need for more color on those steep slopes where the lush green native plants are now doing so well with very little water and keeping the erosion to a minimum.

The landscape committee has no need to ask advice from the professional landscaper who takes care of the landscape and knows whatever colorful flowers you plant on that steep slope are going to die or get eaten by snails. There is a big turnover on the landscape committee because it is only fun for a while, and most quit when their flowers die and the muddy erosion is flowing like lava over the sidewalks. But fortunately, there are always new self-proclaimed experts waiting to take their place and replace those dead flowers.

Apparently, nobody has really questioned why a landscape committee is necessary, considering the HOA already pays professional landscapers. But that's how it's always been. The landscape committee was most likely formed because condos are popular with retired people who no longer want to take care of large yards and big houses. And for about a year they enjoy the condo life of not having any yard work to do. But many find that they miss the yard work, and the landscape committee fills that void, while they wait for the four o'clock happy hour. Well, not all wait for four o'clock to roll around.

Charlie thought there was probably more to the Pat and Tony story than what Fred told. He knew that if he presented logical reasons to trim the trees, the HOA would agree and trim the overgrown trees or at least let him do it. There didn't seem to be any rational reason for not allowing it, and he remembered his realtor saying the association takes care of those common areas.

Garage Fanatic

The interior of Charlie's condo had recently been painted, and the carpet and tile looked good, so there wasn't that much to do inside, which allowed Charlie to concentrate on his two-car garage. He wasn't one to sit around and do nothing and even if he had a television set and cable, he wouldn't have watched it much. Not only that, Charlie didn't have any stuff to properly fill up a garage to the point where you couldn't possibly park a car in it, so he did something quite unique, he parked his small pickup truck inside the garage. He was such a believer in organized garages that he wrote a book about it and knew it would become a big success which would put him into a financial position where he could become the fiction writer that he inspired to be.

However, an acquaintance pointed out to Charlie that he probably put more importance on garages than the average person. And the acquaintance went on to say, the average person doesn't want to even think about that mess in the garage, which is why most people keep their garage door shut.

Charlie knew the guy was right. He knew that it made much more sense for people to park a thirty or forty thousand-dollar car outside rather than disrupting the two-hundred dollars worth of junk that clutters their garages. And parking outside is also a good way to show off your car if you are trying to impress someone. Charlie often thought his biggest problem was that he was too logical. Well, that was one of his many biggest problems.

As he stands inside his garage, he smiles and shakes his head as he looks at the bare bulb sticking out of the cheap ceramic base just outside the door leading to the kitchen which seems to be standard lighting for garages. The fixture is never mounted in the ceiling where you might think a light should be mounted. Nope, it's always on the wall and real close to the door that leads from the garage into the house where it can easily be hit if you carry a large object like a ladder through that door.

Charlie walks to one of the garage walls and is running his hand over a sloppy drywall joint with rusty nail heads sticking out of the drywall that is yellowed because the walls have never been painted. He glances out and sees his neighbor Lou coming up the driveway.

Lou waves and with a straight face asked, "Petting your walls?"

Charlie laughs, "Hi, Lou."

"I know what you're thinking. Mine's the same way."

Charlie said, "Well, and to make things worse, I'm a clean garage freak."

"I can see that. Where's your stuff? You don't have any stuff. How in the world do you get by without stuff?"

Charlie laughed, "Oh, I gave it all away to my ex wife."

"Damn, I never thought about that. That's one way to have clean garage."

Charlie laughs, "Well, it seemed like a good idea at the time. I just did some stupid things. But, you're not entirely correct about not having any stuff." Charlie points to nine cardboard boxes along his garage wall.

"That's my stuff."

Lou nods, "I see. What's in the mystery boxes?"

"Books, nine hundred books."

"You must be quite a reader."

Charlie laughs, "Well, they're all the same."

"Well, it must be a really good book."

Charlie laughs, "Well, I thought so at the time and being a career garage freak, I figured that I was an expert on garages." Charlie walks over to the first box, removes a book and hands it to Lou, and said, "So, I wrote this book."

Lou takes the book and looks at the cover and reads, "Your Garage from Mess to Mansion." Lou nods his head and continued,

"Wow, a published author. That's great."

"Yeah, I just knew I had a best seller going, even though no publisher would touch it, so I self published a thousand copies. Turns out most people don't give a rat's ass about their garages. But, I did sell fifty copies and gave away about fifty. So, I only have 900 left. And that book you're holding is for you. So now, I only have 899 copies left."

"Well, thank you, looking forward to reading it."

The following day, having never overcome his obsession with garages and armed with two new putty knives, a six inch and a three inch, and a large box of premixed joint compound, Charlie proceeded to clean up the shoddy drywall joints. This also required pounding in several dozen nail heads that didn't quite make it below the surface of the drywall. But you can't really blame the builder for shoddy work. Why should the builders care what the garage looks like since the homeowners don't care?

Charlie wished he could obsess about more important things like world peace or starving kids, but then again, there are others are working on those problems and have figured a way to get paid for it. Those seemly impossible jobs are great jobs, because nobody expects a solution.

So really, if you are in the profession of creating world peace or feeding starving kids, then you will always have a job. And the worst thing you could do would be to actually solve the problem. It's very similar to the jobs Jessie Jackson and Al Sharpton have. If these two ran out of discrimination, they would be out of work. But, Jessie and Al, and several others that work this circuit are good at poking sticks in the fire to keep discrimination going.

These guys just seemed to have found their niche in life, which is apparently a real satisfying feeling for con men. But, it's difficult for Charlie to imagine the job of being an instigator that does not help anybody but themselves. To Charlie, being a discrimination instigator is like being a thief, yet not knowing or perhaps not caring or actually believing that you are not a thief. To Charlie, that makes a thief a more respectable person, for they know they are thieves.

Charlie shook head and hated himself when got off on these tangents of thinking too much about things he can do nothing about. So, he just continued concentrating on his garage as he installed two new fluorescent lights in the ceiling and connected these into the switch that previously operated the bare bulb socket which he removed. He also added electrical outlets above an area where he would eventually put a workbench. Then he patched and textured the holes he had to cut to run the wiring to the new light fixtures.

The garage was wide enough for him to install shelving on one side without interfering with parking two cars inside. After he built the shelves he added floor to ceiling sliding doors to cover the shelving, making it look like a closet. Then he bought five gallons of white paint and painted garage interior.

He picked up two workbench height Melamine cabinet kits that you assemble. One had a single door with shelves and the other had three drawers. He assembled and separated the cabinets. Then he attached two by fours to the cabinet's tops which supported a ten foot Formica countertop. Now he had some storage for the few tools he had and a nice work bench area that was great place to set a beer. He also purchased two swivel-top barstools that fit underneath the countertop.

About six o'clock in the evening, Charlie went to his kitchen and took a glass out of the cabinet. Then he opened the freezer compartment of the refrigerator and brought out a nearly slushy Pabst Draft beer that he had placed there alongside two others about twenty minutes ago. He opened the beer and poured it into the glass and smashed the can with a quick twist for the recycle bin. Though he enjoyed beer, he didn't feel right about spending a lot of money on it, nor did he want to admit to himself that beer was a necessary part of his life, even though he knew it was.

Beer had gotten him through some tough times and continues to get him through the tough times. He started buying six packs of the least expensive beers to find the best, or at least what he considered the best, of the cheapest. And though some tasted quite bad, they weren't wasted. During his beer research project, he stumbled onto a beer that was the absolute cheapest of any at the local super market, and he liked it. The cost to taste ratio was right in his beer budget range.

He could get Pabst Genuine Draft Beer for about ten dollars a case of twenty four and sometimes it was on sale. Not only that, the Pabst Company was giving a three dollar rebate on each case. He never saw anybody else pick up a case of this particular beer, but somebody must be buying it or they wouldn't keep stocking it. Maybe most were embarrassed to be seen buying it so they came in toward closing time. In fact, he did notice that the Mexican laborers, who generally lived in make shift camps in fields, seemed to look down on him as he carried out a case of Pabst Draft. They always seemed to go for the Budweiser. Anyway, with his near icy beer, he went to the garage, opened the large garage door, pulled out a barstool, and started watching the sun go down, which required two more beers.

Juan Carrillo

It was early Saturday morning and Charlie's garage door was wide open, in violation of a very strict HOA law. One of the nice things about his condo was that it was directly at the end of the cul-de-sac, so he had the view of the long street rather than a neighbor's place. It seemed that many of the streets in Ranch Ridge had HOA informants that took it upon themselves to report serious infractions of HOA rules, such as open garage doors, parking in guest parking spaces, dead flowers in a planter, or the particularly grave problem of beach towels temporarily hanging on railings to dry. His street, Canyon Ridge Drive, did not have such an informant, for which he was thankful.

Charlie was sweeping the gutter in front of his driveway which was something he had been doing for years at previous houses. An obsession perhaps, but what many don't realize, or most likely just don't care, is that anything thrown in the gutter ends up in the storm drains. And in the complex that Charlie now lives, eventually ends up on the beach and in the ocean. Charlie believed that litter attracts litter and people hesitate to throw cigarette butts and gum wrappers into a gutter that is clean, but if there is one cigarette butt in the gutter, then it's okay to throw your butt in there.

As he had the dustpan in place and was finishing up the gutter sweep, an older truck slowed, and the driver appeared to be looking for something. As it passed by, Charlie noticed a landscaper's logo on the door. The truck pulled into a guest parking space. A Mexican man, who looked to be in his mid-thirties, sporting a worn Padre's baseball cap, got out of the truck and walked toward Charlie. When the man was within speaking distance, he smiled and said, "I've never seen such a clean garage." Charlie was surprised, for he expected the man to have a Mexican accent, but that wasn't the case.

Charlie smiled and said, "Yeah, I'm sort of a garage freak."

"I'm Juan. Juan Carrillo."

Charlie nodded, "Charlie Moore. So you're an early riser too?"

Juan said, "Yeah, I spend Saturday morning checking the job that my landscapers are doing."

"Your landscapers?" Again Charlie was surprised that this young man was in charge of the landscapers.

"Well, they aren't really my landscapers. We own the company together. They all have a part of it. I suppose I run the company a little different than most bosses because I expect a lot out of my employees so I compensate them, I think very well, and have benefits that few landscape companies have. But my men and women probably work twice as hard as the others, so they earn it."

Charlie said, "That makes a lot of sense." As with anybody you meet for the first time, the first impression is usually correct. And Charlie was impressed with Juan, and not just because he owned the landscape company that took care of all the landscape for the HOA. No, he was impressed because Juan seemed like a real person, which many don't realize, is an asset.

Juan looked into the spotless garage and said, "You put in those cabinets and doors?"

Charlie nodded, "Yeah."

Juan said, "You must be a carpenter."

Charlie smiled and his shook his head, "No, not at all. I don't even have a power saw anymore. Just a hand saw, a hammer, a drill, socket set, and drywall screws. But installing those was quite easy. Come on in I'll show you."

Juan checked the bottom of his boots to make sure they were clean before stepping into the garage and said, "I feel like I should take off my boots."

Charlie laughed as Juan followed him into the garage and stood in front of the large sliding doors. He slid one of the doors open and pointed to a short wall that extended out perpendicular to the garage wall and said, "I just framed this wall and glued it to the floor. It's built like a closet inside your house. So you can see, you don't have to be a carpenter to put this together."

"Well, it's very clever and very professional."

"Thanks."

Juan slid the door shut, "And they slide so smoothly." They walked up to the workbench where Charlie had set his cup of coffee that was nearly empty.

"Juan, you drink coffee? It's too early for a beer I guess. I don't know who made that foolish rule about no beer before noon."

Juan laughed, "Noon? I thought it was five."

Charlie said, "Oh, yeah. I guess that's right. I get those two mixed up."

Juan laughed again and replied, "Yes, I drink coffee."

"Have time for a cup?" Juan nodded and followed Charlie toward the door that led into the kitchen.

Juan said, "I'm going to take off my boots. They might be a little muddy."

"You don't have to do that." Juan went ahead and slipped his boots off and followed Charlie into the condo.

Juan looked around and with a puzzled expression, "Charlie, when are your movers coming?"

Charlie gave Juan a questioning look, "Movers?"

Juan hesitated and embarrassed but finally said, "Well, I just wondered, I mean you don't have much furniture, or any furniture."

Charlie laughed, "Wow, you have eye for detail." Juan felt relieved and smiled. Charlie continued, "But that's not entirely true. I have that plastic patio table out there on the deck. And it has four chairs." Juan laughed.

"Yeah, I can see you went all out on that set." Charlie laughed.

"Go on out on the deck and I'll get the coffee."

Juan was standing at the deck rail and looking at the view when Charlie brought two mugs of coffee and handed him one.

Juan said, "This must be the best view that anyone in Ranch Ridge has."

"I guess. I don't what the others have."

Juan replied, "I don't know either." He hesitated and looked a little sad when he said, "You know I've been working landscape in this complex for five years." Juan hesitated again and seemed to have a lump in throat, but finally continued, "And this is the first time I have ever been inside one of these condos."

Charlie didn't know what to say, so he just took a sip of his coffee and finally said, "Well, I hope it's not the last. And if you come over after that ridiculous noon rule we can shift to beer."

Juan laughed, shook head and said, "I'd like that. Well, I guess I'd better get back to my inspection. On Saturdays I try to finish by noon so I can go over and visit my parents and give them a hand with their yard." He handed Charlie one of his landscaper cards and said, "Just let me know when you open the bar."

Charlie with a thoughtful expression, "You know, that's a good idea. Maybe I'll open a neighborhood bar in the garage. You think the homeowner's association would mind a neon sign out front? Something that maybe just said, Charlie's. Maybe have it flash a bit, but not too gaudy."

Juan replied with a poker face, "No, I don't think that would be a problem. But don't be doing something serious, like hanging a beach towel on your balcony." They both laughed. After Juan drove away Charlie started thinking about Juan's last name and wondering if he was related to Leo Carrillo.

Juan Stops for Beer

Charlie wasn't a person who would say things like, "Let's do lunch sometime," with no intention of ever carrying through. But not knowing Charlie that well, Juan never expected him to call, so he was very surprised when he picked up the phone.

"Juan, this is Charlie. Just wanted you to know the bars going to be open tomorrow if you want to stop by."

"Sounds good."

Charlie considered buying some special beer but he decided to stick with the house beer. He had Juan go out on the deck while he poured each of them a Pabts Draft. Juan was standing at deck rail looking out at the view when Charlie came out and handed him his glass of beer.

Juan held his glass up and said, "Well, here's to your new home and I want you to know I appreciate the invitation."

Charlie toasted Juan, "I'm glad you dropped by. If I get the neighborhood bar going, I'll expect you frequently. Or even if I don't, you're always welcome here."

"Thanks. That means a lot to me."

They quickly finished the first beer and Charlie asked, "Another?" Juan nodded. As they were drinking and looking out at the ranch below, and at about half way through their second beer, Charlie said, "I wondered about something. I know that is the Leo Carrillo ranch down there, and with your last name being Carrillo, is there a relationship?"

Juan smiled, "It's interesting that you brought that up. I've been working at Ranch Ridge for five years, and nobody in this complex, that I know of, has ever made that connection."

Then Juan seemed to be a little misty-eyed and continued, "I doubt that many around here know my last name. Most the people around here think of me as the lead Mexican guy. Of course there's no reason they should even know my last name."

Charlie started thinking he shouldn't have asked the question. It was really none of his business, so he said, "I hope I'm not prying. I didn't really mean to."

Juan shook his head, "No, it's not that. It's just that I was born in the United States and have lived here all of my life. But when I'm working on these jobs, and it's because of the kind of work I do, most people assume that I just swam across the border river a couple years ago. So, you treating me as an equal caught me off guard. You seem like the kind of guy that would treat me the same even if my clothes were still wet from the swim."

Charlie laughed, nodded and replied, "Well, I hope that would be case. But don't be dripping muddy water on my garage floor."

Juan laughed and continued, "So, you having an interest in me and my family's name and inviting me into your home in a complex where I'm working is very unusual, but very nice."

Charlie nodded, "I can see that must be frustrating. Seems like in the military, for me anyway, the ethnic thing is just neutralized because you have to depend on everybody around you. So, I don't think about it when I'm dealing with people. Seems like common sense."

Juan continued, "Well, I try to get my workers to think that way. They tend to have a chip on their shoulders, even though most the people we work for treat us pretty good. And some of my workers think the reason that I have a nice house is because I am a Carrillo and my parents were wealthy. There may be a connection to Leo Carrillo someplace in history, but none that made a financial difference to my immediate family."

Juan takes a sip of beer and continued, "My parents immigrated here legally, struggled, worked hard and saved to buy a house and ensured that their children had a good education and encouraged my brothers and sisters to go to college. They couldn't afford to send us off to a fancy college, but with two years of community college and then the state college and working part time jobs, all of us kids graduated. Father understood what made America great, and he knew how important it was for immigrants to assimilate, speak English, get educated and start acting like Americans instead bringing the culture of poverty and corruption with them."

Juan hesitated, shook his head, and continued, "Oh, I'm sorry. I sort get carried away."

Charlie said, "No, I know exactly what you're saying and it's so true. Your father must of had his act together. He seems to have been in a similar position as the California Japanese who ended up doing quite well."

Juan nodded, "That's right. In fact he worked for a Japanese man and he saw and learned about their culture of hard work and responsible spending. I think my father used many of them as role models."

Charlie held up his empty glass, "Another?" Juan nodded and Charlie went for beer.

Juan said, "You know, this street you live on is very unusual. It seems that people on this street are much friendlier. They even invite me to their block parties. In my neighborhood people come home, go inside or hang out in their backyard. I hardly ever see my neighbors."

Charlie said, "Yeah, I'm starting to notice that. It's like an old fashioned neighborhood, where people used to sit on the front porch and talk to neighbors."

Juan said, "You know before this condo complex was here, my father would take us down into that canyon near the ranch house and said that he was going to buy the ranch someday, all 2,538 acres. He knew exactly how many acres. I don't think he really thought that he could buy it, but he seemed to imply that I would be able to buy it by being a successful American."

Juan took a breath and a sip beer, looked out at the view and continued, "But, as you can see that hasn't happened yet. Although my family didn't benefit financially from Leo Carrillo, I received something much more important from him than money. I looked to him as a role model. And just being around his ranch has been magical for me. I did go college like Leo Carrillo, but I was never a newspaper cartoonist for the San Francisco Examiner or a successful entertainer who was in fifteen major stage plays."

Charlie impressed, "That's amazing. I didn't know he did all that."

Juan nodded and continued, "After doing plays on Broadway he moved to Hollywood and did ninety films. But, what's odd is that most people only know him as Pancho, the sidekick to Duncan Renaldo's Cisco Kid, a television series of the early fifties."

Juan took another sip of beer and continued, "And most don't know that he donated a lot of money to the people of California and encouraged kids to go to college. There seemed to be a mystical side to Leo Carrillo. It was as though he had super powers and could make things happen, and that is the part of him that fascinated me. I wanted to have those super powers."

Charlie kiddingly, "You have those super powers?"

Juan laughed, "It's a work in progress. You think I'm crazy, don't you?"

Charlie smiled, nodded and said, "Yes." Juan laughed.

"Well, you wait. You're lucky to live here. Well, maybe it's not luck. Maybe it was meant to be. Anyway, each morning you should look at that ranch and absorb the atmosphere."

"Absorb?"

"Yes, absorb the freedom and vastness. Breathe it in. It'll make each day go smoothly and good things will happen." Charlie smiled and nodded.

"You always been in the landscape business, Juan?"

Juan said, "When I graduated from college, I became a teacher, but I missed being outdoors and decided a national park ranger would be a good job. I applied several times, but was never selected. I guess everybody wants to be a park ranger. So, I started my own landscaping company. You know, I must be hurting your ears from talking so much."

"No, this has been interesting, and seems like we're pretty much in sync with our beliefs. And I'd rather listen than talk."

Nightmare

It is just after midnight, and Charlie is sleeping peacefully as a crisp breeze flows through the open sliding door and gently moving the blinds. Suddenly, a boom-like sound echoes throughout the condo, startles and wakes Charlie. He jumps out of bed, opens a dresser drawer and pulls out his pistol. He is sweating profusely, then sighs deeply and shakes his head as though he is disgusted at himself. He hasn't had one of these nightmares for quite a while and doesn't know what brought this one on. He seems to remember hearing gunfire or an explosion, but it couldn't have been. As he goes back to sleep he decides the noise must have been a car backfiring.

The next morning he goes out to the garage and presses the garage door button, but the large heavy double door does not open. Then he notices the door is sitting at an angle, with one corner resting on the concrete driveway. The lag screws that had been holding the bracket the springs are connected to, have pulled out of the wooden doorframe. It is no surprise, because lag screws are the worst thing you could use but that's what they always use in garage doors like these. Ideally, the initial installers would have used bolts that would go all the way through the frame with a washer, lock washer and a nut. Charlie is glad that it's Saturday because he wouldn't have been able to get his truck out to go to work.

After breakfast, he is on the outside of the garage using a crowbar to raise the heavy door, and at the same time trying to get scrap two by fours under the door so he can reattach the bracket.

As Charlie is trying to lift the door, Juan happens to be conducting his Saturday inspection and sees Charlie struggling. Juan helped Charlie raise the door into position and they block it up. Juan has a bucket of assorted nuts and bolts in his truck and was able locate two bolts that were long enough to go through the doorframe. After Charlie drills the holes, Juan inserted the bolts through the bracket and doorframe and Charlie put on the washer and lock washer and nut on each bolt and the garage door is back in operation.

It was a temporary fix because the bracket on the other side could go at anytime. Charlie started inspecting the wooden garage door, he notices the wood is dried and cracking. Numerous coats of paint over about fifteen years had masked the deteriorated door that needed to be replaced. He decided he might as well install a new sectional metal door rather than a new outdated heavy wooden one that is no longer used in new construction. It seemed quite logical. But he figured whatever he did would have to be approved by the HOA.

He wrote a letter requesting the HOA board select a sectional door that homeowners could install at their own expense to replace the existing aging doors. The letter described the advantages of the sectional door. Safety was a major item he stressed because the brackets pulling out of the frames or springs breaking could cause injury or damage. He referenced cases where springs had broken and penetrated sheet metal on automobiles and had even injured people. Then Charlie researched garage door companies that carried the new sectional garage doors and included brochures from three local companies that would give a discount in complexes such as Ranch Ridge. Each company even had a stock color that would match the existing condo paint. He sent his request along with the supporting information to the HOA board. They responded with a letter saying they would discuss the request at the next board meeting.

Several weeks later, Charlie attended the board meeting. As he sat patiently, he noticed there were very few homeowners present. He did get one look from the board president and it was not necessarily a friendly, welcome to the meeting look. It was more of a what the hell you doing here, asshole.

The meeting went on for about an hour, mostly discussing violations of the HOA rules by the unruly Canyon People.

And then the president said, "I recommend adjourning the

meeting," and somebody seconded it, with no mention of his garage door request.

Charlie, still sitting, raised his hand, but the president appeared to not notice the hand that was now waving a bit, and finally Charlie blurted out, "What about my garage door proposal?"

Milt Cadbury had been the president of the Ranch Ridge Home Owner's Association since the complex was new. Milt, an arrogant, pot bellied, retired thirty year army sergeant, surmised that Charlie, who he had never seen before, was the originator of that request. Milt said, "We discussed that request as soon as we received it and disapproved it."

Charlie said, "Why?"

"Mr. Moore, you are new to our organization. We are a rule run professional organization with meaningful rules that benefit the entire complex. Not just a select few, such as yourself. The HOA board members do not have to answer to an individual once a decision has been made. We do not have to explain our decisions. However, since you are new to our complex, even though you are merely an owner, and not an HOA officer, I will tell you that it was disapproved because the garage doors within the complex do not need to be replaced. If they do need to be replaced we already have a company that supplies the wooden doors. If we allowed you to install an obnoxious metal door, it would not match the existing uniform wooden doors and cheapen the entire complex. I trust, that in the future you will not question the decisions of the board."

Charlie said, "Did the board members study or even look at the material before they disapproved the idea?"

Milt's face, now a crimson tinge said, "God Damn It. There you go again, questioning a decision of the board. Look, I tried to be nice about this, but you are being difficult and disruptive. The meeting is adjourned."

Charlie and all of the board members except Milt and Roberta left. Roberta, in her early sixties and more than plump, with breasts that hang a bit low and a seductive smile that would turn the stomach of most men said, "Milt, I thought maybe I could help you lock up." He nodded, and she walked to him, rubbed her hand up and down his crotch until she felt the start of hardness, and continued, "I love it when you chew out those Canyon People. It just turns me on." Milt puts on his self-centered smirk as he unzipped his pants and Roberta dropped to her knees. She worked on him for several minutes, looked up pleadingly, “Can we go to the motor home?” He nodded.

Charlie, still determined to get a sectional door, found another condo complex that was in the process of changing over to the new modern doors, and the mixture of old and new doors didn’t distract from the appearance of the complex. Now armed with pictures of the old and new doors at the other complex, he put together a petition for the board to select a sectional door and obtained signatures from over a hundred residents. Still, the board disapproved the request, stating that they would need a signed petition from all 140 units. Charlie knew the renter percentage of the complex was about fifteen percent, which meant 28 places had renters, so it would be impossible to get all 140 signatures. Even if there were no renters, it would still be an impossible task.

Charlie opened his third Pabst Draft to compensate for his frustration and anger over the board’s attitude, or actually Milt’s stance against the modern garage doors, for Milt was obviously running a dictatorship. As he sat on his deck and breathed in the cool fresh air, with what seemed to contain a touch of ocean salt, though that could have been his imagination, he found some peace of mind. He just relaxed as he took in the beauty of the ranch below, allowing him to push the garage door situation to the back of his mind.

Milt's Demise

It was two o'clock in the morning when Milt Cadbury was awakened by an extremely loud noise that seemed to come from his garage. Milt yelled out, "Those god damn skate boarders. I'm going to put a stop to this right now." He grabbed the gun belt that holstered his Colt 45 that he had stolen from the Army and strapped it around his waist. Well, he strapped it around a portion of his flabby body that hadn't be well defined for countless years, so the gun belt just sort of hung below his fat gut, and what held it up was a mystery. Then he wobbled down the stairs and stopped at the door just off the kitchen that led to the garage. He pulled the Colt from the holster; quietly unlocked the dead-lock bolt, slowly opened the door, and ventured into the garage where his Mercedes and his wife's Chevy were parked. With the Colt in his right hand, he flipped on the garage light with his other hand.

Milt's eyes were bugged out and his massive mouth dropped open as he yelled, "What the fuck have they done now?"

Some type of projectile was imbedded in the windshield of his car. He knew those little bastards were still in there. He figured they must have hid before he closed the garage door for the evening. He jacked a shell into the chamber, and the sound from the slide action seemed to echo though out the garage. Milt smirked, as he pictured those little snivelers wetting their pants while his bare feet tip toed between the cars.

As he approached the rear of the cars, he felt something sharp enter his right foot and he simultaneously let out a yell, "God Damn it." He looked down to shattered glass covering the garage floor, then looked up and saw that the rear window of his car was completely shattered. "Jesus Christ. Somebody will pay for this." Satisfied that nobody was in his garage, he went back inside the house. He didn't want to disturb the evidence of the crime scene as he trudged back to bed.

The next morning Milt awakens, thinking he dreamed about the vandalism, but then he looked down and saw he still had his gun belt around his waist. He bitched to his wife, who had her own bedroom, and then after breakfast went out to open the garage door to pick up the newspaper. But when he pushed the button, the large garage door did not open. Milt walked to the heavy door and sees that one of the large springs that assist in opening the garage door had broken in half and catapulted through the rear window of his Mercedes and imbedded itself in the windshield.

Then he recalled the request last week from that new trouble making homeowner to install modern safer doors. He can't let anybody know about this incident for he knew the importance of curtailing new people's ideas. They come into his community thinking they know how to do things better. He'd been through this before with the new assholes, and found that they generally cower within a short time, and stop interfering in the complex operation of what he calls, my HOA.

Milt located a telephone number on a curdled up sticker that was attached to the fifteen-year old garage door and called for service on a faulty spring. By not letting the service manager off the phone, the guy finally agreed to replace the spring free of charge, just to get rid of the son of a bitch.

Later that day, after the garage door technician replaced the spring, the technician recommended that Milt have the other spring replaced also.

Milt said, "Would that be free too?"

The technician shook his head and said, "No sir, sorry. That wouldn't be covered."

Milt smirked, glanced over at the other spring and rudely said, "I didn't just fall off the turnip truck. It looks fine to me. You guys kill me trying to squeeze money out of us Nam vets and fixed income seniors struggling to get by."

The technician glanced at the Mercedes again, and fortunately for Milt, the satisfaction of seeing the damage one last time was enough to prevent him from smashing Milt's face with the broken spring that he was holding. He knew he had to leave quickly before that extremely thin layer of wanting satisfaction wore off.

As the technician was getting into his truck, Milt yelled a parting message, "I also plan to file a claim case against your company for the damage to my car."

The technician just shook his head and muttered to himself, "What an asshole."

Milt ran the door up and down several times and was pleased how well it operated. In fact, since the technician lubricated the moving sections of the brackets it was much quieter and worked like new. He was particularly pleased his condo was isolated enough to prevent neighbors from knowing anything about this incident.

Milt slept well that night, knowing that he didn't allow that technician to take advantage of him and woke about eight the next morning quite refreshed. He almost had a smile, or more of an arrogant smirk, as he walked down the stairs. He pressed the coffee maker button and went to the garage and pressed the garage door opener and the door opened quietly and smoothly. Milt pressed the button and the door closed quietly and smoothly. Then he pushed the button again and it opened quietly and smoothly. Milt smiled to himself and thought about the young snot-nosed technician kid that tried to squeeze more money out of him.

Milt was also smiling because he and his wife Emma, a teacher who was on her spring break, were taking off in their motor home for a week in Yuma, Arizona to meet up with his snow bird friends, or perhaps acquaintances would be a better term, for Milt is not encumbered with friends. And it's no surprise that he has a sixty foot motor home, for he is a role model motor-home, motor-mouth kind of person. Whenever he pulls into a motor home park, the first thing he does is find somebody to talk to so he can tell them how well his portfolio is doing and how good deal he got on his motor home. And he is capable of spewing out this dribble while jingling coins in his pocket. It's quite an amazing feat. You kind of have to see it to believe it. Though most people would find Milt annoying or arrogant, he gets along well the true motor-home crowd because most of them did not listen to his bullshit, for they are always thinking about what they are going to say next about themselves. So it works out since everybody talks and nobody listens.

The pleasant motor home people only tolerate him and others like him until they can find another park or a Von's parking lot. Yuma tends to be one of those places where motor-home motor-mouths congregate for motor-mouth competition.

The first time you see Milt's wife, you wonder how someone like Milt could have such a nice wife. Not only is she nice, she is very attractive and in great shape. Few would guess that she is forty-five years old, and maintains her youth by walking and playing tennis. She has a demeanor to match that attractive physical appearance. Unlike Milt, who is a loud-mouth bastard, she is very quiet and seemly shy.

The two of them met when Milt, an army sergeant at the time, was stationed at the personnel office at Fort Ord, an army base near Monterey, California. Her husband, an army helicopter pilot, with twenty one years in the army, was reported missing in action in Vietnam. The Government never compensated her because they couldn't verify that he was dead. They claimed he might have gone AWOL, which was obviously only assumed on their part.

Milt was in charge of submitting paperwork for getting her military compensation. He spent a lot of time and meetings with her regarding the situation. Emma was close to a mental breakdown over her husband's death and the government's refusal to help her get through this tragedy. She had reached a point when Milt seemed to be the only one that cared. He caught her at a weak point in her life and through his pestering and persistence of continuously asking her to marry him, he eventually wore her down.

Even after you know the story about why Milt has such a nice wife, you still wonder how someone like Milt has such a nice wife.

Emma hated the Yuma trips, but she really couldn't complain about her life because she was quite independent. She has her teaching career, and was always doing things like taking college courses and spending time with a few of her women friends from church and playing tennis. Fortunately, Milt had no use for church or anybody associated with church, and he felt that tennis was a woman's game. So she considered going on the Yuma trip once a year, a small price to pay for an otherwise independent life.

The Yuma trip was a only a week, for Milt wore out his welcome quite rapidly, but for Emma a week in Yuma was like a month, then they were finally on their way home where she could return to her normal routine. As they drove into the condo complex and approached the street their condo was on, they noticed water running down the gutter toward the storm drain.

Milt shook his head and said, "What the hell?"

As they pulled into the driveway of their condo, they encountered a stream of water coming at them. Milt said, "Those god damn landscapers have that sprinkler system fucked up again." Milt pressed the remote garage door opener and the door did not open.

Milt said, "Oh fuck, that god damn punk technician screwed up that garage door. I leave town for few days and the god damn place turns to shit."

Milt went into the condo through the front door and then out the door that led from the kitchen to the garage. When he turned on the garage light, he looked down and saw he was standing in a puddle of water. In disbelief, he watched water shooting out the side of the brand new water heater that he had installed just a month ago.

"God damn it. Whatever happened to quality?" Then he looked closer and saw that something was sticking through the side of the water heater. "What the hell." Then he looked even closer through the spray of water and it appeared to be a rusty black spring looking thing. "What the fuck?" Then he realized it was the garage door spring. "God damn it, an inferior spring. That little shit head installed an inferior spring. And I'll bet he did it on purpose."

Then he heard Emma, who had come in just after him. "I thought they replaced the spring on the left. It's still in place."

Milt, abruptly "No, it was, well, I guess so. But by god, I'm going to get to the bottom of this. Something ain't right."

Emma just shook her head and went inside. Milt looked at the paper work and noted the technician had written that the customer refused the recommendation to replace the other spring. Milt, talking to himself said, "That little fucker sabotaged that perfectly good spring."

Even though the water heater was in the garage, the entire wall next to the water heater had become saturated with water and the saturation continued into the kitchen, soaking the drywall and the oak flooring. One wall, part of the floor and some lower cabinets would have to be replaced.

Later, Milt was going through the association mailbox and came upon another letter from that Charlie Moore guy, requesting the concrete steps next to his condo be repaired because the concrete is crumbling making it a safety hazard.

Milt mumbles to himself, "That arrogant asshole homeowner doesn't know when to stop. He's going to find out that he's fucking with the wrong person."

Milt's face is red and he's shaking as he yells, "All this shit is happening because of that asshole." Milt crumbled up the request and threw it away.

Since Charlie didn't hear anything regarding the concrete step request, he is forced to go the next homeowner's meeting. As usual, he was the only homeowner among the HOA officers. Again they discussed infractions and a landscape idea and then Milt closed the meeting. They were probably upset that Charlie was there and they couldn't discuss ways to make the Canyon People miserable.

Charlie raised his hand and asked, "What is the status of my request to have the concrete steps on the side of my condo repaired?"

Milt, impatiently, "We determined it wasn't necessary."

"Well, it is a safety hazard."

Milt's face was getting red, "God damn it, the only people who use those side stairways are the Mexicans. If one of those Wetbacks is so clumsy they slip down that stairway and break their fucking neck, then we'll just get another Mexican. Hell, they're all over the God damn place."

Charlie just went home and had few beers, while Roberta stayed back and helped Milt lock up and then raised her eyebrows and asked, "Motor Home?" Milt nodded.

Your Job is Secure

Most United States military complexes have government supervisors and workers called civil service personal. Perhaps at one time, the civil service actually did the work on projects that are assigned by the Federal Government, but now they generally hire outside contractors to do the work while they supervise. Charlie works as a technical writer at a Marine base for Technical Electronic and Mechanical (TEAM), a civilian company. TEAM liked hiring retired military. Though Charlie was a navy seal for the last fifteen years of his navy career, he had also been an electronics technician and became an exceptional technical writer.

It wasn't Charlie's intention be a technical writer when he retired from the military, nor did he show his religious side often. But certain experiences had turned him into a believer, and one of his most recent prayers to God was that he would make a living as writer when he retired from the military. Charlie wished he had been more specific. He wanted to be a fiction writer, not a technical writer. But it is what it is, and it pays the bills. He enjoyed working for TEAM, because they had incredibly talented engineers and other dedicated professionals. Not only that, he was able to work with the Marines who were also involved in the system development and testing and being around those motivated young men and women marines was refreshing.

However, the civil service project manager and many of the civil service support people on this particular project and throughout the development of the system had unfounded mistrust of contractors. Yet they themselves could not do the job, for they had no applicable skills, which accounts for hiring outside contractors. This negative attitude toward contractors made working conditions stressful.

TEAM contracted to build a Mexican border control system for the Government. The Government had several companies throughout the years working on various border control projects. But apparently only as lip service to the individual states and voters. They never intended for any of these projects to be successful. TEAM developed a system that was ahead of schedule and was actually promising to be a viable border control system. The system consisted of a single tower set up in each state that bordered Mexico. The towers in each state were to be connected together by satellite communications and capable of detecting ground or air activity along the entire Mexican air and ground border. Each border state would be able to monitor their entire state border from one monitor station, allowing them to detect activity and take action with planes, helicopters or land vehicles. The system was being tested using a tower in California and one in Arizona and looking quite promising.

However, the Federal Government was not pleased with the unexpected progress of the system, for they felt that it would affect relations with the Mexican Government, who had become dependent on the money that the thousands of undocumented Mexican workers send back to Mexico.

Not only that, the United States had become dependent on these low wage workers. Oh, and not to be forgotten, the Federal Government failed to mention these undocumented workers might eventually become voters, for many states didn't worry a whole lot about the voter requirement of a being citizen. With such a promising project, the Government could not allow it to continue, so they cut the funding.

However, the civil service personal who were assigned to this project were not affected, for they were set for life. In fact, ten new civil service personal that had been added for this project were also set for life. Shortly after the Government's decision to cut the project, they notified TEAM's corporate office who sent out two guys in suits who must have been recruited from a shady used car dealer, to reassure the employees that the rumors of a layoff were completely false. The employees knew these guys as, Hit Men. The Hit Men have assembled all of TEAM's employees for a meeting. Charlie was sitting next to Nick, a co-worker.

Hit Man 1, who had the brightest sport coat said, "We know there are rumors going around that our corporate office is shutting down this remote department. We don't know how these rumors started, and they are, I assure you, merely rumors. All your jobs are secure despite the Government cutback of defense spending. The sensitive project all of you extremely talented employees are working on is vital to the defense of the United States."

Charlie looked over at Nick and whispered, "That's not good news."

Nick, whispered, "No, it's not."

Charlie shrugged, "Don't give up on them so soon." Nick nodded in agreement.

The hit men spent three days telling everybody that everything was going to be fine. Most of the employees didn't believe this, but they still did their job, partially because nearly all of them had pride and integrity, believed in the project, and best of all, it made the days go faster. A month after the hit men left, Charlie and everybody else was out of a job.

Charlie smiled and said, "See, Nick all that worry for nothing."

Nick replied, "Yeah, they say only ten percent of the things you worry about come true."

Getting laid off upset a few of the employees, but Charlie wasn't one of them. He enjoyed working on the project with the TEAM people and marines, but the government civil service employees made working conditions miserable. And it seemed to Charlie that the civil service manager was using the company as a scapegoat for anything that went wrong. By hiring contractors to do their job for them, there is no chance that anything can be their fault.

It had been a long time since he had a vacation. He was ecstatic when they said they were shutting down his division even though he really didn't know if his finances were going to hold up. Though Charlie wasn't in the best of financial condition, at least his condo loan was his only payment, for he had no credit card balance, no automobile loan and he had always been quite frugal. With the severance pay and selling his vacation time, he had enough money to go for six months without working. Since he was retired from the military he had military health insurance which meant quite a lot, even though he never used it. In his divorce agreement he agreed to give his wife all of his military retirement for three years, but he was able to collect unemployment insurance for a short time.

Charlie's condo had a second bedroom with its own bath so this room would make the perfect rental, which would rent for at least $400 a month. Considering this rent would be tax free money, $400 is like $550 in wages when you take into account federal and state tax, social security, Medicare, medical, and other miscellaneous items that are taken from a check. So renting a room would give him extra time for the job market to open up. But he enjoyed being by himself so he wasn't in a hurry to have a renter. Besides, he also had the income from his Pabst Draft three dollar rebates coming in quite regularly. He chuckled as he wondered if the rebates were taxable.

Bow Saw Serenade

Remembering the story his next door neighbor, Fred Rice told him about the older couple that trimmed their trees to sell their condo and paid a two thousand dollar fine, Charlie decided to take a different approach, since he couldn't afford a fine for cutting trees. He suspected the older couple might have created animosity with the association.

Not that he had been doing much better with his previous requests, but he had to at least give it a try. He drafted another letter to the HOA, requesting that the acacia trees be trimmed to restore the view that the canyon homeowners had paid for. He stated the original amount of each canyon house and referenced some bylaws stating that the HOA is responsible for taking care of the common area behind the canyon condos.

But as he read his letter, he knew that Milt had no interest in making the view or anything else any better for the Canyon People. So he changed the letter to read the acacia trees were harboring mice and rats that use the branches to get up on the roof and into the attics and become a health hazard.

Going through the association mailbox, Milt saw the name Charlie Moore, which set his head shaking so violently you'd think the letter had ruined his whole day, and it may well have, considering what he had been through. He muttered, "That mother fucking bastard didn't learn his lesson."

Milt had the HOA secretary draw up a disapproval letter. Milt knew that this rejection should put an end this Charlie "Fuckin" Moore guy trying to disrupt his smooth running organization.

Milt hadn't noticed that some of his acacia branches had started reaching out toward the eves of his own condo. At midnight the following week he heard noises coming through the ceiling, and yelled out, "Those little bastards are on my roof." He strapped on his Colt 45 picked up his six-cell flashlight and quietly sneaked out the front door. He shined the light on the roof and couldn't see anybody. Then he quickly, or as quickly as his flabby ass would allow, went around to the back of the house. Now he saw the tree branches extending onto the roof.

He muttered to himself, "So that's how those little fuckers got up there. He blasted a light from his six-cell flashlight to the roof and yelled, "Get your asses down here now." There was no reply. But then his light beam came across a pair of eyes glaring at him. He muttered to himself. "It's that god damn neighbor's cat that shits in my flower bed. As long as I'm out here I'm going to take care of it." He picked up a large rock from his flower bed and lobbed it at what he thought was a cat. He missed, but the critter scampered from the roof through a small opening in the eves to the safety of Milt's attic, where a rat's family of babies were tucked comfortably in a nest made of soft insulation.

Milt smiled, thinking that the cat had jumped down from the roof, muttered to himself, "Fucking cat." He was satisfied that the cat was gone and he slept peacefully, as did the litter of baby rats, despite the noise of two adult rats that were busy making more rats for Milt's attic.

Vacation Time

Charlie was enjoying being out of work. This was his first time without a job since he was about sixteen, and it gave him a lot of time to write and think. He quickly adapted to his new schedule of leisurely eating breakfast, drinking a coffee, and taking a run on the beach and a swim in the Pacific Ocean that had an average temperature of 62 degrees, but got all the way up to 68 degrees in August. It was cold and often violent with undertow that could carry you out to sea. But, there was something peaceful about being beat around by the ocean.

It also allowed him more time outside on his deck, which gave him a tremendous amount of peacefulness as he took in the view, breathed in the cool crisp air, and watched the wildlife. This pleasure was only disturbed by those pesky acacia trees that seemed to intentionally reach out with their taunting rapidly growing branches. However, the branches had not yet made an appearance as a nightmare. He chuckled to himself a bit as he wondered how seemingly innocent trees could bother him so much. What was that song that was so popular about a tree? Oh, yeah, a lemon tree. Lemon tree very pretty, but the fruit of the lemon is impossible to eat.

Like most people, Charlie liked the small hardware stores that are quickly disappearing, and the small town close by had one of these nearly extinct stores. It was almost like free entertainment to go into the local Ace Hardware store, though Charlie generally didn't buy anything. He'd often just wander though the store to get ideas.

However, on this particular day, a bow saw, a curved device with a saw blade that can be used with one hand, caught his eye. It wasn't exactly on his budget, for it was nearly twenty dollars. A purchase in this price range, well any purchase for Charlie, was not taken lightly. But something made him go ahead and get the saw.

That evening he needed an extra Pabst Draft to sooth his buyer's remorse. He really didn't need the saw. At least he kept the receipt so he could take it back because he probably wasn't going to use it.

It was about seven in the evening the next day and Charlie had his multipurpose table on his deck. He was half way down his third beer, at which point he was known to get quite insightful. He noticed that the area directly behind the canyon condos seemed to be isolated, and he had never seen any landscape committee people snooping around back there. Nor had he seen any regular civilians down there. So, he started thinking nobody will even know if he takes down a few branches of those overbearing trees. And, he now had the bow saw, and being out of work he had the time. Besides, who is going to miss a couple of branches? Who is going to miss just the ones that are trying to provide a startup bridge that would allow the rats to gain entry to his condo?

The next morning Charlie decided to trim a few sample branches that were reaching onto his deck to keep the rats from getting any ideas about coming aboard the deck. The condo was built on the side of a hill. To get to the back where the trees are you could either go through one of the lower bedrooms or take the concrete stairs down a slope on the side of the condo. Charlie cut a few branches and carried them to the base of the concrete steps and stacked them in a pile. After what seemed like a short time, the pile was getting quite large.

However, as he trimmed one of the acacia trees that had new green foliage on the outside, he discovered that the new growth had been concealing dead branches inside. So he now had one acacia that was no longer very green. In fact, it was just plain real dead-looking brown. But from his experience, he knew the trimming was actually helping the tree and new foliage would quickly fill in and make the tree much healthier.

With the huge pile at the base of the steps, which was hidden from the street, he realized that he needed a plan to get rid of the evidence. He could cut the branches into small pieces and bag it up for the garbage, but it would take a lot of time and bags, and an informant might see the bags and wonder why that condo had so much trash. The city garbage workers probably had a bag limit that had been written into their union contract.

He could have called Juan to help him, but he didn't want to put him in jeopardy on this caper. The best solution that he could think of was to load the branches into his truck and take the load to the landfill, which was only about five miles away. So he backed his pickup into the driveway and carried the branches up the stairs and threw them into the bed of his pickup. Since each load, regardless of the amount, cost ten dollars it made sense to fill the truck with as much as possible. The truck bed was only half full so he backed the truck into the garage for the night.

The next morning he woke to sunshine beaming into his bedroom. Just the few branches he had cut made such a difference. He started making his coffee while doing his morning exercises and then moved his table to the deck to enjoy more sun that was now able to get though.

As he drank coffee, he studied the acacia that he had trimmed, and though it looked quite odd and quite dead, he had trimmed enough trees to know that new foliage would grow back quickly. Since the remaining branches were dead anyway, it would look better if he cut those too.

After breakfast he put on his cutoff jeans, a clean black tee-shirt and his combat boots. Now feeling like a lumberjack, he walked down the concrete stairs with the bow saw and started removing the dead branches of the acacia until it was about a foot off the ground, and obviously no longer stood out. He visualized his neatly trimmed tree sprouting new lush green growth within a short time, and turning into a healthy new plant.

He looked over at a second tree and reached up as far as he could and started sawing a branch that was about three-inches in diameter and extended up about fifteen feet into the air. He was getting into this lumberjack project. He cut a little over halfway through the branch and heard a loud crack and then the branch started falling. As he quickly moved away from the bottom of the tree, he stood and watched the limb come crashing to the ground. He smiled and felt even more like a lumberjack. The cut branch, was so large that it looked more like a tree than a limb.

He cut the large limb into sections and carried each one to the bottom of the steps that went up to the street level. While up there, he decided to go inside the condo to get a glass of water and stepped out onto the deck to view his trimming progress.

With a surprised expression he muttered to himself, “Jesus, that’s quite a hole.” It wasn’t as subtle as he had hoped it would be, since the tree center was made up of dead branches.

He quickly recovered from his disappointment when he looked out above the ranch house and could see a mountain range that was tipped with snow and his view of the ocean had greatly expanded.

His truck was still backed into the garage, so he just pulled it forward far enough so he could add the three sections of the large branch. Then he went back to work with the bow saw and took down another large branch which he hauled up the concrete stairs and loaded into the truck. It was nearly lunch time so he backed the truck into the garage and shut the garage door so he wouldn’t be advertising his truck load.

Just a little later, he pulled an icy beer out of the refrigerator and filled a glass and took a sip. Then he made himself his normal baloney sandwich on wheat. He had previously made a large bowl of potato salad that he had been eating on for several days. He took the final potato salad, sandwich and the beer out to the deck, sat down and put his feet up on a chair. As he looked over his trimming work, his eyes shifted to the expanded view that he now had. This was amazing, he could see the ocean and snow at the same time. Now, he was committed this to this mission and subtle was no longer an option.

As he ate, he identified one more branch that would further improve his view, but it was on Fred’s property. Yet, it was interfering with Fred’s view as well as his own. He didn’t think Fred would care, or probably wouldn’t even notice if he hacked it off. In fact Fred had seen him trimming one afternoon and said he would help but he was on his way to the gym to work out. Fred was not a workout kind of guy, but Charlie believed that Fred was going to the gym, maybe to check out the babes, or shoot the bull, but certainly not to do any serious workout. At least Fred wasn’t part of the HOA conspiracy, nor was any Canyon Dweller that he knew of. But, he wouldn’t put it past Milt to put a renter down here as an undercover informant.

Oh Shit

Charlie had just hauled an armful of branches to the bottom of the concrete stairs and happened to look up. He didn't know how long she had been standing there, and he didn't know who she was. He did know, she did not live on Canyon View Drive.

Apparently she had been walking on the front sidewalk and happened to look down the concrete stairs on the side of the condo. He looked up at her for a brief moment, imagining how he must look with his bow saw in his hand and dust stained sweat running from his forehead. He felt a sinking feeling in his gut, realizing that he had been nabbed by an HOA spy, informant, or snitch. Thoughts were running through his head, not how to get out of the situation, but how he was going to pay five hundred dollars for the first tree and whether or not he would have to pay for some trimming on the second tree. Maybe he would get a discount or maybe they would prorate the second tree, considering he didn't take it all the way down. Or maybe they wouldn't know that he had already removed one tree completely.

He wondered why she didn't say or do something. Then he realized how he must look with the sweat and dirt running off his face, a wet tee shirt, and a threatening saw in his hand. What did he expect her to do? Was she supposed to casually walk down the stairs and give a seemingly madman a subpoena to appear in the HOA court?

Should she have said, "Pardon me sir, but this subpoena is for you." But, as soon as she saw him looking at her, she quickly turned and rushed away. Charlie ran to the bottom of the stairs and slowly stepped up to the street level, but she was nearly half way down the street and apparently going for reinforcements and they would return for the lynching. He did notice, even from a distance, she looked quite nice from the rear. He craned his neck to extend his view. Yeah, she had a great looking ass. Watching her walk away almost made him forget his dire situation.

Landscape Gestapo

Emma had no interest in the HOA, but reluctantly agreed to be on the landscape committee to pacify Milt, who wanted her to keep an eye the other members of the committee to make sure they didn't violate any of the unwritten rules that fit his agenda.

She was a little out of breath, but slowed her pace when she saw the other women on the committee about a block away. They were studying a serious violation of a beach towel hanging from a patio railing and writing a citation that came with a twenty dollar fine for the first offense.

Roberta, the senior officer of the committee, saw Emma coming and said, "Watch what you say girls the gold diggers coming," implying that Emma married Milt for his money.

However, the group was quite upset that Emma had joined their committee because they found it difficult to criticize and gossip about others, not knowing where Emma stood on disliking people or thinking she might report everything that was said to her husband. Since Emma was the newest member, they assigned her to Canyon View Drive to keep her away from the group. Emma liked the assignment because she couldn't stand being around those prissy women for very long.

Martha, a fat, plump-faced woman in her sixties, said, "I know; she struts around like she is some kind of princess. I don't trust her at all."

Annabel, tall, most likely lesbian, in her late forties said, "You know she hangs around with that Mary. And they both wear those little short tennis skirts that women their age have no business wearing. It's quite revolting."

As Emma approached the group, Martha has a big phony smile on her face and said, "Oh, Emma, we thought the canyon had swallowed you up."

Rita, the youngest of the group and very attractive, but was learning bad habits from the others said, "Yes, or one of those canyon dwellers clubbed you carried you off."

Emma shook her head, "No, everything's quiet on the canyon front."

The Waiting Game

Charlie decided to lay low for a few days and wait for the HOA injustice system to take its course or come for him. For seven days, he rushed to the mailbox expecting a summons or a fine or something, but nothing appeared. He hated this waiting and unknown punishment hanging over his head. He figured they must be dreaming up some unique punishment to ensure nothing like this ever happens again. He might have to get a renter right away to pay the fine.

Each morning he sits on his deck and looked through the hole that he created by completely removing one tree. Then he looked at the remaining trees and visualizes the spectacular view that must lay beyond them. Though tempted to return to attacking the overgrown trees, he shifted his focus by working in the garage with the large garage door open, a serious offense, but this allowed him to be on the lookout for the mystery woman. Oddly, he was no longer afraid that she would come back. No, now he was afraid that she wouldn't come back. Regardless of how often he blatantly left his garage open, she didn't show. He thought about buying a shovel and digging some holes in the small front yard lawn to flush her out, or worse yet, hang a beach towel on his balcony.

After a week of not seeing her or getting a summons or bill from the HOA, Charlie was drawn back to the trees. Though he pretended it was the view he was after, he knew there was more to it than that. His focus had shifted and he was willing to chance a serious fine just to get another look at her. This mind-set was chipping away at the simple life he had created. He figured a few more barefoot beach runs during the day and a few Pabst Drafts in the afternoon would cure him of this temporary imposition. But he just couldn't get her out of his mind. He knew what he had to do to get another chance to see her.

The next morning, he slipped into his tree cutting attire, and grabbed his saw. He didn't plan on doing any serious trimming. He would just to trim a little more of the second tree so the hole left from that major branch did not look quite as obvious. But the saw seemed to have a mind of its own as he climbed up into the tree and trimmed around the hole and managed to effectively top the second tree. Even though he didn't cut much off, the dead area seemed to burst proudly out, allowing the tree to reveal its ugly side. In just a couple hours, he had a large enough pile at the base of the steps for a land fill run.

He started hauling the trimmings up the side stairs to his truck bed thinking that that it might flush her out. He took two more loads to the landfill, traveling down streets within the condo complex that were not necessary to go down. It was as though he was trolling for her, using trimmings as a lure, with absolutely no regard for logic or common sense or a huge fine. But he knew this reckless behavior would come and bite him.

About an hour later, upon returning, he started trimming again and while carrying an armful of trimmings, he spotted some movement on the narrow trail that ran behind the canyon condos. Then he saw her, and she briefly glanced at him, but this time she didn't turn and walk away immediately. This was the closest that he had seen her, and she looked just as good from the front as she did from the rear, causing a stirring inside him.

He didn't want to stare, but he did, and then wished he hadn't, because she suddenly turned around and quickly walked away in the direction she came from. He rushed quietly down to the trail to catch a final view of her backside moving through the brush. He thought about following her, but realized it probably wasn't a great idea. Not only that, the mystery of these encounters seemed to enhance the intrigue.

President's Wife

She was a classy woman who didn't allow being over forty to be an excuse for letting herself go. She had filled out with just enough to give her that womanly look and held it because she stayed active by walking and playing tennis. To Charlie, her appearance was only part of the attraction, for there was something else that made her special. Perhaps it was merely the mystery of only getting short glances that intrigued him, or the mysterious ways that she would show up and not take any action against him.

Charlie was no longer interested in looking at young women. As he aged, what he considered attractive, aged along with him like a parallel track. For him it seemed to be a natural progression, perhaps brought on by the appreciation of maturity, or rationalization or merely accepting reality that he couldn't get a young chick anyway. Yet, it was an easy progression and a comforting and secure feeling.

The next day he returned to his project, and as he stood there deciding where to trim next, he spotted her coming up the trail. After making eye contact with him she slowed, but then continued approaching and was soon within ten feet of him and still coming. The closer she got the better she looked.

"You know you're not supposed to trim those trees."

Charlie liked her voice, and let it ring in his mind for several seconds. He hesitated for what seemed like too long, for he didn't know what to say, but finally managed a sort of weak, "Yeah, I know.

When I bought the place the realtor said the homeowner's association would trim them for me. But it doesn't appear to be the case. They just seemed to need a little pruning."

With a doubtful expression, she shook her head, "A little pruning?"

He shrugged as though he knew he'd been nabbed and said, "I'm Charlie, Charlie Moore."

"I'm Emma. Emma Cadbury."

Charlie's mouth sort of fell open and he was thinking, "Oh shit," but finally said, "Cadbury? Are you related to the homeowner's association president? His daughter?"

Emma smiled and replied, "I'm his wife."

"Wow, I guess I am in trouble."

"Well, not because I'm his wife, but being on the landscape committee makes it difficult for me."

"Why haven't you reported me?"

"Well, at first I didn't want you to get into trouble."

"Did something change?"

"I don't know. I've never reported anybody before. But I've never come across a person that seemed intent on taking out the entire forest. And that saw you're using is not exactly a friendly looking device."

"Yeah, I guess I got carried away."

"I was hoping you would stop trimming. But when you stopped, I was hoping you would start again. Maybe I'm reminiscing."

"Reminiscing?"

Emma laughed and continued, "Well, when I was growing up, my brothers took care of our yard and did yard work for neighbors. Sometimes I'd help them. Now, nobody seems to do their own yard work." Emma was relieved and very surprised that she was able to come up with that almost believable explanation.

"So, I remind you of your brothers?"

Nodding slowly, "Yeah, maybe, I think so." She looked into his eyes for several seconds and continued, "Well, maybe the incident reminds me of my brothers."

Charlie hesitated and then said, "So Emma, is inspecting landscape your full time job?"

She laughed, "Well, it isn't supposed to be. But, you've made things a little difficult for me. I've been spending a lot of time keeping the other landscape members from finding out about you."

"Finding out about me? You mean you want me for yourself."

Emma laughed, "Yeah, I want to make this bust by myself so I'll get all of the credit."

Charlie, holding back a grin, put his hands together, "Do you have handcuffs?"

"No, stupid. Look, I don't want to report you, but you're violating association rules. I can't keep covering for you."

"I'm sorry. I didn't mean to make your job difficult. Is there any way I could make it up to you? Like maybe take you to a movie?"

Emma, with a very confused expression, "A movie? Take me to a movie? Are you crazy?"

He shrugged, hesitated, but finally said, "I don't know, maybe. You don't like movies?"'

Emma shook her head, laughed, "Of course I like movies. It's just that we weren't even talking about movies. We were talking about association violations. What brought that up?"

"Well, I mean you ever go to the movies?"

Emma getting a little impatient, "Sometimes my girl friends and I go. But, I'm just curious. What brought that up?"

"Well, I'm going to a movie today. I just wanted to let you to know that I won't be working here this afternoon. I don't want you to make a special trip all the way down here."

Emma laughed but found herself upset because he didn't seem to be the kind of guy that would go to the movies by himself. He must have a wife or girlfriend. What bothered her, was that she found herself jealous, as though she had found this lumberjack and didn't want to share him.

She did her best to shrug off the feeling and said, "Well, it might surprise you, but I have other things I do. I don't spend my entire day inspecting for landscape violations."

Then she paused for a while, not knowing what else to say, but finally, "So you just take off in the middle of the day and go to the movies?"

"No, not usually. There's just a movie that sounds interesting. The theatre is off University Avenue. Not such a great area, but the theatre specializes in offbeat films. Stuff that you won't see at the local theatres."

"So this must be some special movie."

"It's a French film called, 'The Lover' and starts at two. There's a small bookstore near the theatre that has coffee and it's kind of neat little shop. Anyway I'm going to be at that bookstore about 1:15 and head over to the theatre about 1:50. Charlie continued, "Did you use to go to the movies with your brothers?"

Emma was relieved when he said he would be there by himself, but she seemed somewhat frightened because he seemed to be sort of hinting around for her to go with him. No, she thought, it was much more than a hint. He was asking her to go with him, and she was frightened because she considered the offer, yet knew she wouldn't go. She was just happy that he wasn't going to be with someone else.

But then she remembered his question and responded, "Oh, the movie with my brothers? Well, yeah. There was a matinee on Saturdays that we went to sometimes." She nodded, "Yeah, I forgot about that. But why are you telling me what time the movie starts?"

"I don't know. I just thought you might happen to be in the area."

"Yeah, sure I will. What a coincidence" She shook her head and laughed. "No, I doubt that I'll happen to be driving down University in an area that is not so great looking. And I have no intentions of going to a theatre that shows a film that that sounds a lot like a porno movie."

Nodding understandingly, "Yeah, I guess that is a stretch. But you never know."

Emma, nervously looked at her watch and said, "Oh, it's getting late I have to get going." She went up the side concrete stairway, and as she was walking toward her condo, she glanced back and saw that Charlie was at the top of the steps watching her.

She wondered what kind of person goes to the movies in the afternoon. And why doesn't he have a job? And why tell her about going to see one of those kind of movies? When she got home she picked up the movie section of the newspaper and read about the film.

"The Lover is a 1992 drama film based on the semi-autobiographical 1984 novel by Marguerite Duras. The film details the illicit affair between a teenage French girl and a wealthy Chinese man in 1929 Vietnam."

He didn't seem like the kind of guy that would go to a porno movie or if he was he wouldn't admit it, or he certainly wouldn't ask someone to go with him. Milt supposedly had a golf game today and usually didn't get home until six or seven. At noon she took an extra long shower and thought about turning the cold water on herself, but changed her mind and stepped out of the shower.

As she dried, she stood naked in front of a mirror for a while, somewhat disgusted with herself because she had layer of fat on her belly. Still naked, she went into the bedroom and selected a pair of brief panties that she only wore for special occasions, and then struggled to pull on her black Levies and then slipped a white sweater over her head. Then she started worrying, or perhaps had a touch of jealousy that he might have called someone else to go with him since she didn't accept. Yet, on the other hand, it seemed like an open ended invitation. Then she shook her head as she realized that this is ridiculous. She was behaving like a high school girl.

She unzipped her Levies and started to pull them down over her brief panties, and as she glanced in the full length bedroom mirror, she could see the crack of her ass through the transparent nylon of her panties. She smiled, and wondered if she was still sexy, and that thought generated a sensual sensation. She just shook her head as she stupidly felt like a young girl knowing she had to snap out of this ridiculous infatuation. She started stepping out her tight jeans. But then, wiggled back into them.

Porno in the Afternoon

He is sitting at a round table in the corner reading a book and sipping a cup of coffee as she walks up to him and said, "Hi." She couldn't tell if he was surprised that she came.

But he smiled and was obviously glad to see her as he stood and put his hand on her shoulder and said, "Hi."

"Just happened to be in the neighborhood."

"Yeah, you never know when that'll happen. I'm glad. I don't really like going to the movies by myself."

"Well, I didn't know that. You should have said something."

He smiled and nodded, "Want a coffee?"

"No, I'm okay."

There were only about fifteen people in the theatre which wasn't surprising considering it was afternoon and the middle of the week. Emma glanced over at some of the patrons as they walked down the aisle. She did see one other couple and then two women sitting together, thinking they were probably gay because this area of San Diego County had a large population of gays. She started to feel a little more comfortable, and allowed a stirring of anticipation to flow.

She is thinking she had never been to a porno movie before. Not that she thought this was a porno movie, but then she started wondering and really didn't know what to expect. Maybe it was considered a porno movie. However, what she did know, was that she hadn't felt this stimulated since her college days.

Charlie said, “Where do you want to sit?”

“Oh, I don’t care as long as it’s not the front row.”

The film starts playing, “A fifteen year old girl and her family are French, but live in Vietnam where her mother is a schoolteacher. Her mother and two brothers live in across the Mekong River and the girl attends a school that is on the other side of the river. She is a loner but an excellent student, who dreams of being a writer.”

“She meets a Chinaman when crossing the river on the ferry after a school holiday ended. He is the son of a wealthy Chinese businessman, and has recently returned from Paris after dropping out of school. He has the look but lacks the self-assurance of the playboy he fancies himself to be, and he is mesmerized the first time he sees her standing by the rail on a crowded ferry crossing the Mekong River. After some awkward conversation, he offers her a ride to Saigon in his chauffeur-driven limousine and she accepts, although the two barely speak during the drive.”

“The Girl tells the Chinaman she is 17. The following day, he waits for her outside her boarding school, and the two go to the room he rents for entertaining mistresses in the seedy Chinese quarter, where they make love. They realize that a future together is unthinkable because she is scheduled to return to Paris soon, and his marriage to a Chinese heiress has been arranged. Aware of the limited time they have together, they fall into a relationship in which they shed all responsibilities that come with commitment. Every day after school, the girl goes to the bachelor room.”

Charlie and Emma’s shoulders were snug against each other, partly because this was a very old theatre with seats that were close together and partly because both seemed to encourage the snugness as the film played on. Their arms rested against each other on the armrests and a few times during the film she leaned close to his ear and whispered something about the film and Charlie breathed in her pleasurable scent.

“The girl’s family discovers the affair, and though at first angry, they encourage her to continue because the Chinaman is wealthy and able to pay off some of their debts. The Chinaman falls in love with the Girl and begs his father to be allowed to marry the girl instead of his arranged marriage, but his father would rather see him dead than with a white girl. Though both devastated, the Chinaman marries his arranged bride, and the girl boards a ship days later to return to France.

Decades later, the girl is a successful writer. The Chinaman telephones her, as he is visiting France with his wife. He assures her that he never stopped loving her, and that he would not stop for the rest of his life."

The film turned out to be more erotic than porn and a good story. But, it did have some racy scenes, which further complicated Emma's emotional situation. She really didn't need any additional encouragement for her feelings toward this stranger. This worried her, but felt so nice that the worry was worth the risk. And maybe the risk was part of the pleasure.

As they walked out of the theatre, Emma said, "What'd you think of the movie?"

"I liked it. At first it was a little disturbing the way he initially treated her, and her family's reaction wasn't what I would have expected. But I suppose, it was realistic since they needed money."

She said, "Yeah, the family surprised me too. Sometimes French films are too strange for my tastes. They generally take forever to move a story along, but this one was just right."

Charlie asked, "You want to get a cup of coffee or a drink."

She looked at him and her eyes were a little misty. "Oh, no thanks. It sounds good, but I'd better get home."

She wasn't anxious to leave him and walked slowly, stalling and waiting for him to encourage her to stay, knowing she probably would have given in. They brushed against each other several times as they walked to her car. And she was shaking as she pulled her keys from her purse, causing them to slip out of her hand onto to the sidewalk.

Charlie picked them up, and she managed to unlock the car door. Then she sighed, gave him very brief hug and said, "Thanks for the movie. It was a nice day for me."

She started to open the car door, but then turns to Charlie and said, "You know, I do have time for a coffee."

As they walked back toward the theater they came upon a bar called, BAB'S. Charlie looked at Emma, and with a straight face said, "Been in here before?"

She casually said, "Oh, it's been a couple weeks." He laughed. He liked her quick wit.

BAB'S fit into the area quite nicely because it looked like a dive on the outside, yet upon entering, and once their eyes adjusted to the dim lights, it wasn't quite that bad on the inside. There was some odor of stale cigarette smoke but less than what you would have expected. A woman bartender was talking to four older men who were sitting at the end of the bar. One was wearing a suit.

The bartender looked up and waved. Charlie and Emma walked up to the bar and the bartender approached. She smiled and said, "What'll you folks have?"

Charlie looked at Emma and she said, "Just a glass of white wine."

Charlie said, "I'll have a beer, draft's fine."

They took their drinks and walked to a small round table in a corner. Their knees were touching as they take a sip of their drinks. As they looked into each other's eyes, each felt a craving that they had not experienced in a long time.

"I'm glad you came."

"Did you think I would?"

"I don't know. I guess I just hoped."

"Doing this is definitely not something I would normally do. I mean, I have never done anything like this before. I mean sitting in bar in the afternoon with a stranger."

"Stranger? I feel like we've been seeing each other for nearly a month."

She shook her head, and with sort of a serious look said, "No, I don't want you to get the wrong idea, Charlie. It's just movie and drink."

They were nearly finished with their drinks when Charlie said, "Would you like to dance?"

"Dance? What brought that up?"

"I don't know. You mean dancing didn't enter your mind?"

Emma laughed, "No, surprisingly not. No, it didn't. You know you're kind of weird, Charlie."

"Yeah, I know. But I'm struggling."

"Struggling?"

"Yeah, struggling to stretch out the time with you."

Charlie gets up and walks to the jukebox that most likely hadn't been played for quite a while since the buttons were dusty. He studies the listings and then slips in a coin and pushes A4 and a song starts playing:

"Desperado, why don't you come to your senses?
You been out riding fences for so long now
Oh, you're a hard one

I know that you got your reasons
These things that are pleasing you
Can hurt you somehow"

Charlie returns to the table and puts his hand gently on Emma's shoulder and said, "Can I have this dance?"

"Don' you draw the queen of diamonds, boy
She'll beat you if she's able
You know the queen of hearts is always your best bet."

Emma smiles and stands, and he took her hand as they walk to the small dance floor. He puts his arm around her waist and they start dancing as the music continues.

"Now it seems to me, some fine things
Have been laid upon your table
But you only want the ones that you can't get"

Emma said, "I haven't heard this song for a long time. Can't remember what it's called."

Charlie whispered in her ear, "Desperado, sung by the Eagles but Patsy Cline wrote it."She pulls herself into him a little tighter.

"Desperado, oh, you ain't getting no younger
Your pain and your hunger, they're drivin' you home
And freedom, oh freedom well, that's just some people talking
Your prison is walking through this world all alone."

He whispers, "I'm not much of a dancer. Suppose I don't have to tell you that. A successful dance for me is not stepping on your feet."

She puts her head on his shoulder, sighs and whispers in his ear, "You're doing fine. I would say much too fine."

"Don't your feet get cold in the winter time?
The sky won't snow and the sun won't shine
It's hard to tell the night time from the day
You're losing all your highs and lows
Ain't it funny how the feeling goes away?"

Juan Comes to Dinner

Charlie woke a little earlier than usual, but lay in bed for a while thinking of Emma and how nice yesterday was. Everything seemed to be falling into place. He smiled to himself when he thought about his situation of being unemployed, struggling financially, and being attracted to a married woman who had a screwy, psychotic bastard as a husband, yet he felt so content. Not only that, the sun was starting to shine though the window of the bedroom.

He had oatmeal and toast and an egg for breakfast and headed out to trim some more branches. As the day progressed, noon came and she hadn't stopped by yet, so he kept trimming until about one o'clock.

He remembered her saying, "Charlie, it's just a movie and a drink." But she said that before the dance. So, it was more than a movie and drink. What about the dance? But now he realized that he was being stupid and too optimistic. He knew there was no logical reason why she would get involved with an unemployed guy who was kind of a loser and a weirdo that goes to questionable movies in the afternoon. All Charlie could possibly get out his efforts would be a huge fine from the HOA. Not only that, if she wasn't satisfied with her life with that bastard, then she would have left him a long time ago.

He carried the morning trimmings to his truck and then went inside the condo and out to his deck with a beer, which he finished quickly and got another. As he sat looking at the newly expanded view, he realized that it didn't mean as much to him now. He allowed someone into his life that meant something to him, in direct violation of his rule of keeping things simple. And now, the view has blurred.

He had known guys who could date and be with several women at the same time. He knew that they would just shrug off a woman that walked away and merely move on to another. Why couldn't he be that way? It seemed like he made things harder than they should be, yet he thrived on simplicity. His previously simple life had been made more complex. Now he wished yesterday had not happened. He was disgusted with himself for bringing on more baggage.

God, he disliked himself when his mind zigzagged with these overwhelming thoughts. He got another beer and then another and then laid down and slept until three o'clock and drove a load of trimmings to the landfill.

The following morning he started trimming again and she didn't show up. After lunch he drove to Del Mar Beach and ran barefoot in the sand much further than he had run in a long time. Then he took a plunge into the icy and choppy ocean where he body surfed and let the powerful ocean beat him around and almost wished the undertow would pull him out to sea and put an end to his misery.

He knew there were only enough branches left for one more day of trimming and he could have completed the job, but he had been holding back, not wanting to finish, because she might show up. He just needed a little more time to forget about her. He needed something to get her out of his mind so he invited Juan over for dinner and some conversation.

Juan said, "So, when you asked me to dinner, I thought you'd at least be taking me to a nice restaurant."

Charlie laughed, "You're not going to get a burger and baked potato and steamed fresh peeled carrots as good as these in a restaurant. And not even the finest restaurant this side of the continental divide will be serving Pabst Draft in a cracked glass that only leaks a little."

Juan laughed, "Yeah, can't argue with that." Then he took a bite of his hamburger and a sip of beer and continued, "You said you wanted to talk about something."

"I guess. I don't know. It's about a woman."

"That's a relief. At least you won't be hitting on me."

Charlie, very solemnly, shakes head and slowly, "Well, don't rule that out completely."

Juan laughed, "Well, I'm no expert on women. Who is she?"

"Well, her name is Emma."

Juan, almost snorted his beer up his nose, takes on a shocked expression, and starts shaking his head, "Oh, no, Charlie. No, that's not a good choice. Look, if you need a married woman, I have this neighbor. I know she would like you a lot. She seems to be attracted to tree trimmers."

Charlie smiles and can't help but chuckle, "What you got, a dating service on the side? No wonder they don't accept you in your neighborhood. It has nothing to do you being a God damn Mexican."

Juan laughs, "She's just a very friendly neighbor that has a husband that travels a lot."

"Look Juan, this isn't something I planned. The problem is, she stopped coming around."

Juan sighed, "Well, that's good. She knows what's best for both of you. She's a smart lady."

Charlie nods with an unhappy expression, "Yeah, I guess you're right."

Surrender of Emma

Charlie was up early the next day and by noon had trimmed enough for two loads. After lunch he was back at it. It was nearly four o'clock when he finally wrapped up the job and was looking it over. Then as he started up the side stairs, he looked up and she was standing there. They stood looking at each other for what seemed like a long time, and his eyes started fogging over, when he finally said, "God, I missed you."

"I missed you too. I tried not to come." She walked down to the bottom of the stairs and stood close him. As she looked into his eyes, she saw that tears had mixed with the dirt on his face. She took her thumb and carefully wiped away some dirt near his eyes. Her eyes were moist, "Are you okay?"

He shook his head, "No."

She could see and feel his sincerity as she nodded, hugged him, and whispered, "I know. It will be okay." Then she backed away and said, "It looks like you're finished. I mean you're out of trees. You'd be cutting dirt pretty soon."

Charlie said, "Yeah, it's amazing the damage you can do with the little saw that could."

She smiled, "You're a real mess. I want to help you clean up."

Charlie, puzzled, "Help me clean up?"

"Yeah."

"Well, I only have this bow saw. It's the only tool that I have."

"No, I mean I want to help you clean up. I want to wash your back in the shower."

Charlie was stunned, not knowing what to say. He just stood there looking puzzled for several seconds but finally blurted, "That'd be swell."

She smiled, "Swell? You're such a master of words Charlie."

She followed him into the garage and as they stood near the workbench, he reluctantly said, "I ah, usually take my clothes off out here. I mean so I don't track dirt through the house."

She shrugged indifferently, holding back a grin, "Need help?"

"Oh, no I just didn't want to, or I just wanted to tell you, or warn you or something. But I guess I should just shut up and close the garage door."

She said, "Okay. Yeah, that's a swell idea." She backed away a little and waits.

He said, "I'm not very good at this."

"If you were good at this, I probably wouldn't like you."

He untied his boots, slipped them off, removed his socks and she slipped off her shoes and removed her tee shirt.

She moved in closer and said, "I don't know what it is about you and I don't know what is happening to me, but it doesn't seem to be anything I can control. And I don't really want to control it." Her bra was against his bare chest and she reached down and unbuttoned his cut off jeans and slowly slipped the zipper down while she looked into his eyes and said, "Your face is so tan and so dirty."

She backed away a little, and waited as he slowly pulled down his jeans and she took off her shorts. Now as she stands in just panties and bra asked, "Do you take off your underwear too?"

"Oh no, not out here."

She put her fingers between the waistband of his underwear and his stomach and said, "Well, I just wondered because they are quite sweaty and there seems to be some dirt in the waistband."

He said, "That's okay." He put his hand on her back, guided her through the door into the kitchen and watched the movement of her silk panties that seemed like fine translucent wrapping paper that allowed her ass cheeks to peek through.

He washed his hands and took two tall glasses from the cabinet and filled them with ice and then water and handed her one. He drank his quickly, refilled it and she sipped some of hers. They took their water and walked through the living room.

She said, "What a spectacular view. It must be beautiful at night."

Charlie nodded, "Yeah, too bad I've never had a chance to share it with anybody."

As they walked down the stairs toward the bedroom he said, "You can use that bathroom in there if you need to. I'll start the shower in here." He pulled the blinds that he normally left open and then turned on the shower and heard the toilet in the other bathroom flush.

He had just stepped out of his underwear when she came in and said, "Would you help me with this bra?"

She turned her back to him and he nervously fumbled with the bra hook until the thing finally gave up the traditional fight and unhooked. He slipped the bra from her shoulders and she pulled her panties down. She had him go into the shower, and as he was facing the spray of water, he heard the door shut and felt her body lightly pressing against his backside. And her movements against him, as she washed his back, were quite stimulating for both of them. Her washcloth moved from his back to his chest and down to his stomach. And though trying to be subtle, in no time she reached much lower and may have stroked the hardening member a little more than necessary to complete the wash. Then she said, "I hope you didn't take that wrong, I'm just cleaning you up. It's included in the wash." He smiled, turned around and said, "That was nice."

They kissed and he asked, "When was the last time you had your back washed?"

"I don't know. I guess when I was a young child in a bathtub. I don't remember. I've never had a shower with anyone before. I mean except in gym class with girls."

He smiled and said, "Oh, really."

She laughed, shook her head, "No, not like that."

She looked down between his legs, shook her head with a doubtful look, and said, "I don't know if you'll be able to get close enough to wash my back."

Charlie laughed as she turned around and faced the showerhead then put her head under the water, and he was surprised that she didn't worry about getting her hair wet. He soaped the washcloth and started gently washing her back and then moved the washcloth down each cheek of her ass and continued down her thighs and each leg.

He moved closer to her until he was pressed against her backside. He reached around with a soapy hand and touched one of her breasts, causing her to back into him a little more tightly.

She said, "That feels so good. You know Charlie; you could make a living just washing backs."

She pulled away from him a little, turned and faced him and they kissed.

She said, "Have time for a nap?"

"I don't have anything planned."

She said, "I can feel something that has a plan."

He laughed, "I tried to talk him down."

"Well, if you multiply that length by two, you will know how I feel."

They stood under the shower and kissed as the water peppered down and rinsed the soap off. Then Charlie got out of the shower, put a bath towel around himself and took Emma's hand as she stepped out. She turned her back to him and he put the towel around her shoulders, and she could feel his hardness against her backside. They laid on the bed and kissed gently at first and then more anxiously, as they knew where they wanted to go.

Both were breathing heavily when they separated and were facing each other. Emma smiled, "I thought you said your bow saw was your only tool." He shook his head and smiled then kissed her. Then she took on a serious expression, and almost teary eyed, "I didn't remember how nice it could be. I've been miserable the last two days. I know that this is a bad idea. I just couldn't come up with a better solution. This isn't something I do all of the time. I mean this isn't something that I've ever done."

"Oh, I didn't know. I just thought this was part of the homeowner's association welcoming package."

She laughed, "You know that's a good idea. I'll have to bring it up at the next homeowner's meeting."

"Well, if it was assigned by committee, I'd probably end up with Roberta standing at my door."

She laughed, "I'm just sorry that you ran out of trees to trim. As you can see it's built up my appetite."

"Well, I do have painting in the garage to do."

A quick response, "That'll work." She kissed him and said, "Can I ask you something?"

" I don't know. You could give a try."

"How did you get those scars?"

"Oh, I had my appendix taken out."

She nodded, "That must have been a very large appendix."

"Yeah, doctor said it was biggest he had ever seen."

"Why are there so many different scars?"

"Well, the doctor had never done an appendectomy before, so he wasn't exactly sure where it was located."

"Come on Charlie. I'm not leaving till I get an answer."

"I was hoping you'd say that."

Charlie kisses her and they make love again. Afterwards, she asked, "What branch were you in?"

"Navy, a navy seal." Charlie's eyes are watery.

Emma wipes the moisture from his eyes and kisses each eye and hugs him.

"I'm sorry Charlie."

"Ah, it's okay. It's nothing I don't think about every day anyway. Where was Milt stationed in Vietnam? I've never been close enough to him to read his cap."

"Oh, he was never there. He handled so many service records and was involved with writing up combat awards. I think he lived vicariously through the service files of the solders that were there. He was good at writing up combat awards for others and himself, but not good at getting my Government settlement. I've just given up on that."

"You don't seem to be a good match for Milt."

"Well, when they came to the door and told me my husband was missing in action, the Government couldn't confirm he was dead, so they couldn't start any survivor payments. Milt was the sergeant in charge of the base personnel office and was helping me get a settlement. He was the only one who took a personal interest in my situation. It seemed like he was the only one that cared. I guess he was infatuated with me and wore me down."

"I didn't mean to pry. It's really none of my business."

She kissed him, "That's okay. It's a natural question. Most people are afraid to ask." Then she said, "You, know I have get going."

He nodded, "Thanks for helping me clean up."

"Keep your garage door open for me."

"Isn't that against the association rules?"

She replied, "I think we just decided to ignore all the rules." Then she dressed and sneaked out the bedroom patio door and hastily started walking down the trail behind the canyon condos. As she walked, she fluffed her damp hair and trying to make it presentable.

After walking a distance from Charlie's place she walked up the slope to the street level when she heard someone say, "Been swimming, Emma?" There was no mistaking Martha's raspy irritating voice. It almost seemed they had been shadowing her. She wouldn't put that past them.

Emma forced a weak smile and said, "Somebody down there has a sprinkler going and I wasn't paying attention." Martha snickered a bit and held fast to a smug, suspicious look.

"Well, we missed you at the last landscape patrol. We didn't have anybody to cover the canyon." Emma shrugged and just kept walking to her home.

Next Day

Milt is hitting golf balls on an area of specially grown and manicured grass that is actually association property, but he has everyone believing it is part of his property. Roberta happens to walk by. Well, happens to walk by on purpose and seductively says, "Well, hello Milt." Milt nods and waves. Roberta continues her babbling, "Your bride seems to be spending a lot of time at the canyon."

He scowls, "What do you mean?"

"Oh, nothing. She's doing such a fine job on the landscape committee. Then Roberta raised her eyebrows and said, "She handles the canyon you know. But it's quite odd though. I mean she hasn't written any citations since she's started. And, as you well know, those people down there, particularly that one gentleman, are far from perfect."

A half hour later Milt is alone in his bedroom thinking that Emma should be home from the landscape patrol by now. Then he develops a suspicious expression. He straps on his holster, takes his colt out and ejects the clip, looks at it, and then snaps it back in.

Emma and Charlie are in his bedroom getting dressed. She says, "I'm going to be brave today and sneak out the front door."

They walk upstairs to the front door then kiss and hug. Emma slowly opens the door and looks to see if anyone is watching. She walks out and hurries to the street. Just as Emma is sneaking out the front door, Milt is walking on the lower canyon trail toward Charlie's condo. When he reaches the rear of the condo and sees the four stumps that Charlie has taken to the ground, he mumbles out loud, “What the fuck?” Then he mumbles a little louder, “Jesus Christ.”

Charlie steps out on his upper deck to see who is yelling, and said, “What’s the problem?”

“What’s the fucking problem? You cut down all these god damn trees.”

Charlie sees that Milt is wearing a holster and said, “I’ll be right down.” Charlie goes downstairs to his bedroom, opens his dresser drawer and pulls out his pistol and walks out on his lower level patio with the pistol in his hand.

Milt sees the pistol and sarcastically said, “I hope you have a permit for that thing.”

“I hope you have bullets in that relic you have strapped to your side.”

Milt makes the best squint that he can muster up and said, “Mister, what you call a relic, has gotten me through some tough times.”

Charlie couldn’t resist replying, “Yeah, it’s a rough neighborhood.”

“I’m talking about Nam you son of bitch. I’ve got medals that you could only dream of.”

Charlie continued, “Yeah, I can imagine. You were a yeoman, or whatever the Army calls a typewriter jockey, right? It gave you a lot of time in an air-conditioned office plagiarizing and typing your own recommendations for medals.”

“Why you disrespectful shit head. What the fuck do know about Nam and combat medals?”

“It’s been my experience that anybody that has actually been though combat doesn’t advertise it on a ball cap. Most of us navy seals are trying to forget how we got ours.”

“Navy seal my ass. I’ll bet you spent your time in Canada. You couldn’t make a pimple on my ass.”

“Pimple on your ass. Gee, what an original cliché. What really irks me is when people use worn out phrases like that. But, if you do have pimples on your ass, I’d have Roberta checked.”

“What the fuck you talking about? Why you lying bastard. What else you been doing down here besides illegally cutting down thc association trees?”

“What? The association needs to know my personal life too? That another one of your rules?”

Milt scoffed and said, "One last thing. Don't make me have to come down here again. And by god, you'll severely pay for those trees that you've cut down."

Sheriff Means Business

Later that week, Charlie and Emma are in bed while Roberta and Martha are knocking at the front door of the Cadbury condo. Milt comes to the door and Roberta smiles, "Hi, Milt. We were wondering if your sweet Emma is here. We are starting our landscape tour."

Milt gruffly, "No, she said she was meeting with you."

"Well, maybe she went ahead and started her tour of the canyon. She might be visiting one of the Canyon People. Might be the one that thinks he's above the association rules."

The door slamming shut almost catches Roberta's nose. She is initially stunned, but then a huge grin forms on her face as she hears Milt yelling, "That asshole. That god damn asshole." He stands at the closed door and starts breathing heavily, his eyes are bugged out and his fists are clenched, as he screams, "That son of a bitch."

Within a few minutes, Milt has his ball cap pulled down to his eyes and his Colt strapped to his waist. He is still breathing heavily as he rushes down the street toward Charlie's condo. Out of breath, he just stands at Charlie's front door trying to catch his breath. He pulls out his Colt and makes sure the clip is place and then puts the Colt back in the holster. Sweat is pouring down his face from his fast walk of nearly a block. He ignores the doorbell button and raises his fist to bang on the door, but hesitates. Knowing the bedrooms are downstairs, he changes his mind, and rushes toward the concrete stairway that leads to the lower level.

Milt is now much calmer and his smirk shows a sense of satisfaction as he stands at the top of the stairway, takes out the colt and pulls back the hammer. The sound of the hammer locking back makes him wish Roberta was here to go down on him. There was just something about that hammer locking back. He starts thinking this must be what combat is like. But he knows he won't kill the tree cutting mother fucker. He just wanted to see the arrogant son of a bitch piss himself in front of his wife to show her what a chicken shit he is. And it'll teach that bitch to stay in her own backyard. Then he started wondering who else she has been fucking over the years. He starts talking to himself, "Maybe that piss-ant in Yuma that has that miniature motor home. I'll find out next year. That fucker's always there. I thought he was one of them there homosexuals."

A wicked smile, that seems to come naturally, is imprinted on his face as he starts down the stairs. Suddenly, the deteriorating concrete on the third step, crumbles and Milt's foot slips, sending him tumbling head first down the stairway and the colt discharges.

Charlie and Emma, quickly sit up in bed when they hear the gunshot and a puzzling flopping noise that is the sound of Milt tumbling down the stairway.

Emma terrified, "Oh, my God, what was that?"

Charlie jumps out of bed and puts on his pants and tee shirt and grabs his pistol from the drawer.

"What you doing with that gun?"

Charlie ignores her, runs out the sliding door of his bedroom and then to the side stairway and sees Milt laying at the bottom of the steps with blood rushing from a wound. As he rushes toward him, he is pulling off his tee shirt and yells, "Emma, call an ambulance. There's a man down. He's been shot."

She yells, "A man shot?"

"He yells, "Yes, it's your husband."

He applies his tee shirt to Milt's wound to slow the bleeding and then starts CPR.

Emma is crying and shaking as she makes the call and then puts on Charlie's robe and rushes outside and sees Charlie performing CPR on Milt. The paramedics arrive but Milt doesn't make it.

She is sobbing and mumbling, "Oh, my God, this is all my fault. My God, what have I done?" Charlie goes to Emma, puts his arm around her for comfort but she pulls away and said, “Get away from me. Leave me alone. Just leave me alone.”

A couple hours later, he calls Emma but she hangs up without saying anything. He calls her again that evening but she didn’t answer.

Then a week later he knocks on Emma’s door. Emma comes to the door. He said, “You haven’t answered my calls.”

“No, Charlie. Please stop calling or coming over. I just can’t see you anymore. It hurts too much. Just leave me alone.”

Juan Calls

Charlie answers the telephone, "Charlie, it's Juan. I haven't heard from you for a while. I heard about Milt. Everything okay?"

"Hey Juan, oh yeah things are going good."

"Well you don't sound that convincing. And I've heard some rumors. Sounds like you might be up to a six pack a day or more."

Charlie actually worked up a small chuckle, "Now that's a darn lie. Maybe a six pack, but not more. Well, not more every day."

Juan said, "Well, I thought maybe you could meet me over at the Gypsy Rover. It's in Encinitas. I'll buy you a drink. But, I don't think they serve Pabst Draft."

"Must be real dive, huh?"

Juan is encouraged, because Charlie hasn't entirely lost his sense of humor. He replied, "Let's just say there's no reason to get dressed up for the place."

Juan is sitting at the bar talking with the Rosita, the owner. As Charlie cracks open the door of the Gypsy Rover and his eyes start adjusting to the darkness, he reluctantly inhales the fresh cigarette smoke that sort of combines with the stale cigarette smoke, neither of which cancel each other out.

Juan and several other patrons or perhaps regulars is a more appropriate term, turn toward the open door that allowed a thin slice of sunlight in and you'd think they were going to have to reach for their sunscreen because an inconsiderate bastard let some daylight in.

Charlie approaches Juan, and Rosita, the bar owner, confronts him, "Look mister, we don't want no trouble in here. If you've got a beef with Juan, take it outside."

Charlie takes on a confused look, which is just what she wanted and then she smiled and said, "What do you want honey?"

Charlie shook his head and smiled, which was something he hadn't done in a while, and said, "Whatever he's drinking."

Rosita said, "You want a clean glass or a dirty glass? Clean one's a nickel more."

Charlie shook his head, looked at Juan and said, "You put her up to this huh?" Rosita smiled.

Juan said, "I just wanted to check out your sense of humor. You know, see if you had any left. You didn't sound too happy on the phone."

"I'm okay."

Rosita said, "Su amigo es muy guapo." (Your friend is very handsome.)

Charlie gives Juan a questioning look.

"She said you look like shit."

Rosita gives Juan a dirty look and Charlie nodded and smiled and said, "Thanks Rosita."

They drink their beers down about a half and Juan said, "You ever take a vacation Charlie?"

Charlie looks at his beer for while, develops a thinking expression, before saying, "I've been on vacation since I lost my job."

Juan smiles, shakes head and said, "I don't know if cutting a small forest with a hand saw and only quitting because you ran out of trees and then taking down a dickhead, qualifies as a vacation."

Charlie just nodded, smiled a bit, and finished off the beer.

Juan got Rosita's attention for two more, and continued, "I've been thinking about flying down to Mexico and visiting my cousin. She owns a bar down there. I haven't been down for a while, thought maybe you'd like to come along."

"Don't know if I can afford it. I mean tickets and all."

"Well, there's no ticket involved. I'm going anyway so it's about the same amount of gas."

"You never told me you had a plane."

Juan said, "Just never came up. I think the first time we met was when you had a problem with your garage door. What was I suppose to say when I first met you, something like, I've got a plane and you've got a busted garage door?"

Charlie nodded and smiled, "It seems like I need to get out of here for a while."

Juan said, "So, Emma isn't answering your calls, huh?"

He shakes his head, "No, I don't blame her. Guess I just have to forget about her. Mexico sounds good to me."

Milt's Desk

Emma sits down at Milt's large desk and sighs, thinking that as much as they didn't really get along and he was a jerk, she should have just had the guts to divorce him if she didn't like how things were going. Her mind is fogged over. She had been wandering around the condo and then settled into the worn chair at his large desk in the spare bedroom that had been made into his office. She never spent any time in his office except for the weekly cleaning and dusting. She did her paper grading and school work at the kitchen table.

She randomly slides open an upper file drawer and thumbs through some files and shuts the drawer, and then pulls on the lower file drawer and finds it locked. Her previously unfocused expression turns to an inquisitive, more focused look. She opens the narrow drawer above the file drawers where she thought she might find a key, but pulls it too far and it comes off the track and lands in her lap.

She disgustedly said, "Oh, shit."

As she fumbles to get the drawer back on the track, she hears something clink on the hardwood floor. She sets the drawer aside, looks down and sees a key. She picks the key up and tries it in the locked file drawer and pulls the drawer open. As she randomly thumbs through the files, she sees one labeled, "GOV," which she pulls out and sets on the desk top. As she looks through the documents in the folder, she gets a stunned look on her face. She finds Government papers and settlements for her husband's death and notification of monthly payments of $2,000 a month. She looks at the acceptance papers that were signed when they still lived in Monterey.

It was her name that was signed by somebody other than her, and notarized by a Roberta Pritchett. She continues looking though the drawer and finds a folder containing bank statements from a Monterey bank, which is not the bank that the two of them have for their joint account. And, there are two automatic monthly deposits from the US Treasury going into the Monterey bank. This bank has two separate saving accounts with $2,000 a month going into one and $1,500 a month going into another.

The first one is for her husband's death and it has a balance of a little over $100,000. The other account is for the death of the husband of a woman named Maria Rollins, which has a balance of nearly $200,000.

There is also a monthly allotment of $500 a month going to a Roberta Pritchett and an insurance policy for Roberta Pritchett for $15,000.

Milts army retirement check and her teacher's check are automatically deposited into their joint San Diego account. Emma is starting to get angry as she pieces together these bank statements. She started thinking about the $60,000 motor home that he paid cash for about a year ago. And he always seemed to have money for his Alaskan fishing trips and Wyoming hunting trips he took every year. He said the money came from an inheritance of his uncle who passed away. As she continued through the folder she finds another San Diego bank statement that contains automatic deposits from Ranch Ridge homeowner's association for $1400 a month. This account has $90,000 in it. Emma surmised that he had been taking ten dollars a month from each of the 140 units in Ranch Ridge.

She shakes her head, "Jesus Christ, he should have been a congressman." As she continues through the files she finds yearly tax folders. Even though Emma had been doing her own taxes when she was previously married, she went ahead and let Milt handle it. He apparently made up dummy tax forms for her to sign and then on the tax form he submitted, he forged her signature. When she looked at the tax form that was actually submitted to the IRS, the total income was staggering. She just shook her head, and was thankful that the taxes had been paid on the stolen income. At least the government wouldn't be coming back at her for back taxes.

Despite her initial anger over Milt's scheme, a sense of relief and joy came over her because the guilt she previously felt had vanished, or perhaps turned more to anger and hate, yet even that was overridden by a sense of freedom.

Then, seemingly out of nowhere, the name Bitchy Pritchy popped into her mind. At first this was puzzling, but then she nodded and recalled being part of a group of wives at Fort Ord that had husbands in Vietnam. They would get together and have a few drinks and just try to have good time and not worry for a while. She remembered several of them had spoken and joked about a career army woman that worked in personal who was extremely rude. They called her Bitchy Pritchy. And then she remembered that the acceptance papers to allow her settlements for her husband's death were notarized by a Roberta Pritchett, AKA, "Bitchy Pritchy." Emma just shook her head and realized that Bitchy Pritchy being in the same neighborhood as Milt was no coincidence.

With everything Emma had on Bitchy Pritchy, she could probably have her spend the rest of her life in Leavenworth, the federal prison. But she had no interest in helping the federal government, for they'd screw things up so badly that she'd probably end up in prison herself or in court and have to pay an attorney and they would drag this out for years. Besides, she had enough to do to get this financial mess in order and Bitchy Pritchy would escape prison, but not financial loss.

She had a friend in Monterey who might know where Maria Rollins lived so she could arrange to have the monthly payments that she should have been getting. And she could write a check for the amount that she missed over the years plus interest and a little extra to cover what Milt might have spent of her money, which should be a sizeable tax free amount.

Then she would stop the monthly money that Milt had been siphoning from the HOA and the yearly auditor could determine that the monthly HOA fees could be reduced by ten dollars. Then she could figure out how to subtly repay the amount Milt had embezzled from the HOA.

But first, she had something much more important to do than deal with the Milt's financial folly.

She gave herself a quick look in the mirror, noticed but chose to ignore the dark bags under her eyes, and then hurried out the door toward Charlie's condo. She might have guessed that she'd run into the three stooges, Roberta, Rita and Martha, who are writing a citation on one of the canyon condos that had unauthorized flowerpots on their balcony. Emma was surprised that Roberta was out there and she didn't seem that upset, or even upset at all, about Milt's death. He was probably blackmailing her for helping him cheat his victims, so her loyalty may well have been just an act and now she might be relieved that she didn't have to pretend anymore. And, she might have known about the life insurance. Of course she couldn't know that her allotment would stop, so the $15,000 insurance was not very much for the lying life she had led. But freedom from him and staying out of Leavenworth is not such bad way to end up.

Martha, whose entire demeanor blatantly hints of insincerity said, "Oh, Emma. We are so sorry about Milt. You must be devastated. He was the glue that held the association together. He was our rock."

Emma shook her head in disgust at the phony bullshit and said, "Go Fuck yourself Martha and you too Roberta. Or should I say, Bitchy Pritchy." Roberta gets a paralyzing, fearful expression, but no verbal response as though she has a big dick propping open her mouth, and her jaw hinge is locked the open position.

Emma continues, "And Rita, you're too nice a person to hang around with these bitches. Get some new friends. Come down and play some tennis with me sometime."

Emma continues toward the front door of Charlie's condo, and just as she is raising her hand to knock, for some unknown reason, she changes her mind and rushes for the side stairway. She anxiously starts down the stairs but on the third step, her foot slips on the crumbling concrete and she has a split second vision of Milt tumbling headfirst down the treacherous stairs. At the same time, a smile appears on her face, for she sees Milt's Buddha Belly leading the way to his fate. With a natural movement of her waving arms she manages to fall backward rather than forward. Though she scrapes her back on the edge of the steps and makes a hard landing on her butt, she's smiling. She sighs as she sits on the crumbly step for a minute, just to catch her breath. She just sits there, while feeling the pain and initially thinking maybe this is God's warning to stay away from Charlie.

Then out loud, she said, "No, God, maybe you should share some responsibility for Milt's death. Maybe you should share some responsibility for her falling in love with Charlie. Or maybe you should take some responsibility for me having to put up with that asshole Milt for all these years. It doesn't seem fair, God."

She was proud of herself for standing up to the big guy and despite her butt and back pain she smiled and carefully continued down the stairs and said, "Thanks for listening, God."

Charlie is sitting at his table, with what looked like about a half a dozen empty beer cans pushed aside and a beer in his hand and the bow saw on the table. He hasn't shaved for three days and is staring out at a vast unobstructed view. But she couldn't have known what he was thinking as he sat in a depressed state of mind. Sure, he'd put down a few beers, but he was more depressed than drunk.

She yells up at him, "Charlie, I have to talk to you. Can I come up?"

Charlie is startled out of his trance and slurs ambiguously, "I guess."

She enters the condo through the lower bedroom door, takes the stairs two at a time as she heads toward the upper deck where Charlie is sitting. He doesn't get up, but motions her to have a seat. She gingerly sits on her throbbing butt and then carefully allows her bruised back to rest against the back of the chair.

As she looked at the bow saw that was on the table, it flashed through her mind that the bow saw was a much more powerful weapon than Milt's Colt 45. That Bow Saw took down the Crooked Sheriff of Ranch Ridge.

Charlie slurred, "Want a beer?"

Emma smiles, shakes her head and said, "God Charlie, It's not even noon."

"Well, you know how I am about those association rules."

He held out his hands, "You'll just have to cuff me and take me in."

Emma nods, then smiles, "Yeah, Charlie I know exactly how you are about those rules. Sure, I'll have a beer."

He slurred again, "So, what's so important that you felt inclined to interrupt my happy hour?"

She took a long drink of beer and said, "Remember how I told you Milt was the Sergeant in charge of reviewing and submitting my paper work for military benefits when my husband was killed? Well, it turns out he did submit it and it was approved, and the government has been paying Milt since it happened. Not me, but Milt. And then he made phony letters from the Government saying they couldn't give me benefits because my husband was missing action and possibly a deserter. I continually fought the Government over this but all of my appeals went through Milt."

Charlie, with a sympathetic expression takes Emma's hands and said, "I'm sorry."

"And you know what Charlie, he was collecting money from another woman whose husband was killed. Her name is Maria Rollins and I found out that she still lives in Monterey."

"All those years with that lying bastard. You know Charlie, if you hadn't cut down those trees down, I'd probably never have found out the truth."

He shakes his head slowly, "Emma, I can't take credit for things I've done here."

She's puzzled, "What do you mean, Charlie?"

"I had spiritual guidance from Juan and Leo Carrillo."

She's even more puzzled.

Charlie smiles, takes her hand and guides her inside. "I'll explain after I wash your back."

She undressed and went into the shower before Charlie. When he stepped in, he saw a painful looking scrape on her back and a huge black and blue bruise on her butt. "You're hurt, what happened?"

"Oh, God and I had a misunderstanding. But we worked it out. I'll explain after we wash each other's backs."

Later, they are on their sides looking at each other. Charlie has a concerned expression.

"What's wrong, Charlie?"

"Before you came over today," he hesitated, took a deep breath and his eyes started to moisten as he continued. "Well, I was sitting out there thinking that the view didn't mean anything without you to share it with."

She smiles and rolls over on top of him, and as they were joined together she said, "Charlie, I love you."

Afterwards, they were facing each other and she asked, "How would you like to take a trip to Monterey the long way?"

With a puzzled look, "The long way?"

"Yeah, you get off Highway 101 near San Luis Obispo and pickup Highway 1 to Morro Bay, which is a quaint little town. We could spend the night there and then continue on Highway 1 through Cambria, San Simeon, you know, where Hearst Castle is located and then Carmel is further down the road."

Emma continued, "I still have a couple weeks of summer vacation left and I have to take a check to that very deserving woman who lives in Monterey. We might as well make a vacation out of it. We can make a few stops along the way. I've always wanted to stay at Clint Eastwood's Mission Ranch in Carmel."

Charlie, with a mystified expression, "Clint Eastwood's Ranch? So, we just pull into his ranch and say, "Howdy Clint, just back away, cause we're going to be staying here for a while. Maybe rope some cows and stuff."

She laughed, "Well, a while back, when Clint Eastwood was Mayor of Carmel, some developers were going to tear down the historic buildings of the1800's Mission Ranch that was one of the first dairies in California. It is located right on the ocean, overlooking Point Lobos, a beautiful ocean view. The developers planned to tear down the old buildings that made up the ranch and build a condo complex. Before they could act, Clint bought the entire 22 acres that had a house, barn, and bunkhouse. He had each of the old buildings remodeled and made it into a very quaint place to stay. There's even a restaurant on the property where the locals go. And I've heard that Clint eats there when he's in town, since he lives in that area."

Charlie said, "Sounds swell."

She nods and laughs, "Swell, my gosh Charlie, I knew you'd really be ecstatic about it, but had no idea it would rate a swell."

"Well, sometimes I get a little overwhelmed."

She smiled and nodded.

He continued, "The only problem is that Juan and I were talking about going to Mexico to visit his relative. He wanted me go with him. I guess I feel obligated because he's been a good friend, so I told him I would."

Emma nodded as though she understood, "Oh, that's okay. I can go there by myself and we can do it some other time. I mean if you are still interested in seeing me once in a while."

"Emma, I rather go with you. But I can't or don't know how tell him."

"Well, maybe he would come with us?"

"You serious?"

"Yeah, Juan's a nice guy. Just explain your predicament. Maybe you could work something out or do Mexico with him a little later."

He nods, "Yeah, I'll talk to him."

Later, Charlie is on the phone with Juan. "Juan, I've got a problem."

"Another problem. Charlie, what is it this time? Garage doors, tree cutting, killings, married women, what else can go wrong?" Before Charlie can answer, Juan said, "Oh no, don't tell me you ran out of beer."

Charlie laughs, "No, it's not that serious, but something came up. Emma and I are together again."

"Hey that's great. Glad to hear it. Why is that a problem?"

"Well, she asked me to go up North through Morro Bay and Carmel."

"That's a great idea Charlie."

"But we were wondering if maybe you would like to come along."

"You're kidding me. Why would you want me tagging along?"

"I don't know. Well, you and I sort of made plans to go to Mexico. You've helped me out a lot, and I guess I just value your friendship. I just don't want you to think I'm using you."

"Come on Charlie, true friendships include flexibility and understandability and drinking cheap ass beer. There's no ego bull crap involved in a true friendship. It's not a matter of things like, gee you like her best. Good god, Charlie, we're not in high school. It'll be fine. You think I wouldn't discard you in a second if I had a choice between a wonderful woman like Emma and you? Hell, I'd even choose an un-wonderful woman over you. And you'd understand."

Juan continued, "I'll tell you what, I'll fly to Monterey, rent a car and maybe we could have dinner somewhere together. It's been a long time since I've gotten away. And I like that area."

Heading North

The disadvantage of living in San Diego County, where Ranch Ridge is located, is that you have to drive through Los Angeles County to get to Central and Northern California. As you creep along Highway 5 north and inhale the smog that hangs in the air and tolerate the belligerent buttheads, bullies, and assholes, that attempt to push you down the road using their bumpers, fingers and horns, as they smugly hide inside their beastly sheet metal vehicles, there is one thing that keeps you from going insane.

That one thing, is knowing that the punishment of the drive through Los Angeles County will be rewarded when you break off onto Highway 101 and get a glimpse of the Pacific Ocean and start breathing the cool clean air. Highway 101 runs along the coast for quite a ways and then heads inland which is okay too, for that area is wide open interesting country.

As Emma and Charlie approach San Luis Obispo they are looking for the Highway 1 sign which will take them to Morro Bay.

Morro Bay

If you approach Morro Bay by sea as Juan Cabrillo did in 1542, you'll first see a rock, well actually a huge boulder, that extends upward 576 feet above the entrance to Morro Bay. This boulder is the result of extinct volcanoes. Entering or leaving Morro Bay by sea can be quite challenging and hazardous, as discovered by the actor George C. Scott when he and his wife were aboard Mojo, a chartered a 70 foot boat that was struck by a huge wave near the harbor entrance. The boat was severely damaged. Scott was not hurt but his wife suffered a broken wrist, as the story goes. There seems to be quite a few versions of what happened that day. But, someone managed to snap a spectacular picture of the incident and the picture hangs in many of the Morro Bay shops.

However, if you approach Morro Bay by automobile, which obviously Charlie and Emma have, they didn't have to worry about getting hit by a huge wave. They checked into a nice place to spend the night that was very close to the Embarcadero, a wharf that had been built by a family named Riley and his wife who moved to Morro Bay in 1864 and built the first house and founded the town of Morro Bay.

Charlie and Emma held hands as they walked along the wharf and dropped into a few shops along the way and saw the famous George C. Scott picture. Being nearly noon, they found a restaurant that served fish and chips and beer. After a pitcher of beer and their meal, they strolled back to the motel and took a long shower together. Charlie got out of the shower first and quickly dried himself. When Emma stepped out he put a large bath towel around her. They laid down on the bed facing each other and dosed off to sleep. It was nearly six when they woke.

Hearst Castle

The following day, as they drove along Highway 1 and were near the town of San Simeon, Emma said, "Charlie, did you know that in1919 Randolph Hearst hired Julia Morgan, one of the first women architects, to design a guest house for his ranch at San Simeon. When she finished the guest house, he was so impressed with her work that he had her start designing Hearst Castle. She spent 28 years supervising most of the construction of Hearst Castle."

Charlie said, "She must have been quite an architect or almost as pretty as you." Emma laughed.

As they continue North past Hearst Castle, on highway 1, also called the Pacific Coast Highway, they take in the continuous beautiful scenery and spectacular Pacific coastline and finally reach the Mission Ranch and check into the Honeymoon Suite. The restaurant where they have asked Maria, the woman that Milt stole money from, to meet them at the Mission Ranch Restaurant.

Mission Ranch Restaurant

She was thin, but not a weakly thin, a pretty woman with short dark hair in a very plain but nice dress. You could tell she wasn't the kind to put on act or try to be somebody she wasn't, because it wasn't necessary. Being herself, fit her perfectly. But her face had taken on a worried and puzzled expression as she stood at the restaurant's reception desk, not knowing why she was invited. It was something about her husband who had been missing in action. Though she lived in Monterey, she'd never been to the Mission Ranch before. In fact, she didn't go out much because she no longer had friends in the area. Most of her friends had been Army wives who no longer lived Monterey.

Emma, sitting at a table with Charlie said, "That must be her." She stood and navigated through the tables toward the woman, smiled and asked, "Maria?"

The woman nodded, then Emma hugged her and said, "I'm Emma, let's go sit down." She took Maria's hand, noticing that she wore no rings, and led her to their table.

Emma explained how Sergeant Cadbury had cheated her out of her husband's survivor settlement, and she would start receiving them soon. Then Emma handed her the envelope that contained a cashier's check for $225,000. Maria opened the envelope and looked at the check, shook her head slowly, and tears came to eyes as she said, "Is this real? I don't understand."

Emma took her hand and said, "This is your money. Money that Sergeant Cadbury has been cheating you out of for several years. The taxes have been paid. It's all yours."

She sniffs and dabs her eyes and Emma hands her a tissue. "Oh my gosh. I can't believe it. Are you sure? Is this just a joke?"

Emma, gets choked up and tears form in her eyes, but finally said, "No, Maria, it's true."

"No, it can't be. Are you sure?"

Emma takes her hand, looks into her eyes, nods and said, "It's true, it's real."

"But how? Are you from the Government?"

Emma smiles and said, "No, I'm not from the Government. They have nothing to do with this anymore."

Maria said, "Oh, God."

Then she takes a deep breath, "I can get some new tires for my car. Oh, thank you."

When Maria said, "I can get new tires for my car." Both Emma and Charlie get tears in their eyes.

Then Emma takes Maria's hand, pulls her to her feet, hugs her and said, "Let's go the lady's room and then we'll just enjoy the evening."

Maria, with tears still in her eyes, smiles and nods.

Back at the table, the three of them had just ordered a second round of drinks when Charlie sees Juan at the reception desk. Charlie waves and Juan nods and makes his way to the table.

Charlie stands, shakes Juan's hand and gives him a hug and said, "I'm so glad you made it." Then Emma stands and hugs Juan.

Juan looks down at Maria, smiles and she stands and said, "Hi, I don't know you but I guess a hug won't hurt."

Juan smiles, "I guarantee that a hug from you won't hurt me a bit." She smiles and the two of them conduct quite a lengthy hug for strangers.

The four of them settle back at the table and the waitress is gets a drink order from Juan.

Maria, allowing the drinks to seemingly pry open her personality and curiosity said, "Emma, how did you and Charlie meet?"

Emma said, "Well, it's quite a long story. But it has to do with tree trimming, a porno movie in the afternoon, a dance a little later and the Cisco Kid's sidekick, Pancho."

Maria smiled and humorously said, "Oh, that's perfectly clear."

Emma laughed, and said, "You're too young to know about Pancho. Actually, Charlie and I met while he was trimming trees behind his condo. And I just sort of took a liking to that tree trimming hunk."

Maria smiled, looked at Charlie, nodded as she raised her eyebrows, "Oh, now that is perfectly clear."

Charlie was shaking his head in embarrassment.

Maria said, "How about you Juan? Can you add anything to this mystery? How do you fit into this group?"

Juan nodded and said, "This could take a while to sort out. But you could force some answers out of me. That is if you have the time."

Maria said, "Be careful, I might take you up on that."

As they talked and sipped their drinks, a very tall gentleman in jeans and a casual shirt enters the restaurant. Emma gets an inquisitive look, and whispers, "Is that him?"

The receptionist is smiling and talking with the gentleman, and then he starts walking into the restaurant. As he is walking by their table, he suddenly stops, looks at Charlie with a puzzling expression and said, "Don't I know you from somewhere?"

Charlie nods, "San Juan, Puerto Rico. You were working on the Heartbreak Ridge film and the navy assigned our team to help you out with some shooting and explosions. But I didn't expect you'd remember me."

The tall guy shook his head and said, "I've told too many people about drinking with you and your submarine friend to forget that night." He squinted and continued, "Your friend, he had a strange nickname that's not coming to me."

Charlie smiled, "Scudsey."

The guy nods, "Yeah, we were in the Chief's Club. So, what are you doing here? You're not going to blow anything up, are you?"

Charlie smiled, shook his head, "No, those days are over for me. I'd like you to meet my friend Emma and this is Maria and Juan."

Emma shook his hand and he turned and shook Maria's hand. Then nodded and smiled at Juan.

Maria smiles and said, "Oh, it's so nice to meet you."

He said, "Well, thank you. Same to all of you."

Charlie said, "You have time for a drink with us?"

He nodded and said, "Yeah, but I don't want interrupt your dinner."

Emma said, "Yes, please sit down. I'd like to know about that night in Puerto Rico

I'm sure I'd never get it out of Charlie."

Maria nodded, "Yes, it sounds like an interesting story."

The guy looked at Charlie and Charlie just gave a shrug indicating it was okay.

The guy sat down and said, "Since the ladies don't know the story, I guess I have to fill them in. I came into this Chief's club, looking for some beer and solitude, and as I was walking toward the bar, I walked past two these two chiefs in uniform at a table and I noticed their dolphins and Charlie had dolphins and his seal insignia. I'm always interested in talking to navy chiefs because they seem to have some interesting stories."

Emma looking puzzled, "Dolphins?"

Charlie said, "It's an insignia submariners wear."

The tall guy nodded and said, "I'd never really had chance to talk to many submariners or navy seals and here I had both of them. But I don't remember how you and Scudsey ended up drinking together."

Charlie said. "My first four years in the navy I was on a diesel sub with Scudsey. He and I ran around together. Then I went off to the Seal Team and hadn't seen him for several years. He just happened to be on the sub we were working with so we went out for a few beers."

The guy nodded and said, "Yeah and Scudsey had on these dolphins that had the initials DBF on them so I asked him about that. And he said, 'Diesel Boats Forever.'"

Charlie said, "Yeah, Scudsey loved the diesel boats and wanted to return to them after his shore duty. But he had been an instructor during his shore duty and became an expert on oxygen generators. When his shore duty was over his oxygen generator skill was needed on a nuclear boat that going under the ice."

Maria, very interested asked, "Oxygen generator? It makes oxygen?"

Charlie said, "Well, it breaks down water, separates the hydrogen and the oxygen, and puts the oxygen into the submarine's oxygen banks and discharges the hydrogen overboard. This allows nuclear subs to stay under a long time without coming up for fresh air. It's great for under ice operations."

Maria said, "That's amazing."

The guy nodded and said, "And what an interesting fellow. Your friend Scudsey starts telling about his love of diesel submarines as opposed to nuclear subs." He said nuclear power has ruined the submarine service."

"I asked him what the difference was, and he said, 'A whole lot of things. But take terminology for instance. On a diesel boat, they're shit tanks, but on a nuclear sub, the same tank is a sanitary tank. And nuclear subs don't have a garbage disposal unit. Oh no, nuclear subs have a trash disposal unit. It's the same darn unit.'"

The guy hesitated and smiled, "And then Scudsey said, 'Near as I can figure, you can take a fellow off some Midwest farm, send them to nuclear power school, and he no longer takes a poop. No, now he has Bowel Movement.'"

Emma and Maria started laughing, and Juan was smiling, and the guy looked relieved because the story was a little crude.

Charlie nodded, "That about sums up Scudsey. He's a classic submarine sailor."

The guy nodded, "That was a great night, and you know, having a drink with you ladies and men is very special to me also. Well, I hate to run but I guess I'd better get on that piano. It was really nice meeting you ladies, Juan and seeing you again Charlie."

Maria said, "Piano?"

"Yeah, they find out I'm in town and drag me down here to play. I pretend like it's an inconvenience, but I actually enjoy it. Then he added, "Maria, can I play something special for you?"

Maria, completely caught off guard, and a little embarrassed, but pleased, "Oh, gosh, I don't know, oh wait, I know, how about, Misty?"

He said, "I was hoping you'd say that." He got up walked to the piano and started playing and singing.

Look at me.
I'm as helpless as a kitten up a tree.
And I feel like I'm clingin' to a cloud.
I can' t understand.
I get misty, just holding your hand.

Juan said, "Maria, would you like to dance?"

Mara glances at Emma with that raised eyebrow questioning look, Emma smiled and nods and Maria said, "It's been such a long time. You sure you want to chance it?"

Juan said, "I'm no Fred Astaire, but we can chance it together."

Maria smiles and they make their way to the dance floor.

Walk my way,
And a thousand violins begin to play,
Or it might be the sound of your hello,
That music I hear,
I get misty, the moment you're near.

Charlie raised his eyebrows at Emma and said, "Would you like to dance?"

Emma said, "Of course, if you promise not to blow anything up." Charlie smiled and nodded.

Can't you see that you're leading me on?
And it's just what I want you to do.
Don't you notice how hopelessly I'm lost.
That's why I'm following you.

As they danced, Emma whispered in his ear, "Charlie, this seems to be Maria's night, huh."

Charlie nodded and said, "Well, it's about time. She's certainly earned it."

Emma said, 'You crying, Charlie?"

He sighed, "Naw, well yeah, guess I am. Being with you and good friends, this trip and the evening and dancing, it's a little overwhelming. Yeah guess I am"

On my own.
When I wander through this wonderland alone,.
Never knowing my right foot from my left
My hat from my glove
I'm too misty, and too much in love.

Bunkhouse

About midnight, the four of them leave the restaurant and walk with Maria to her car. Emma and Charlie give her a hug and then Juan gives her a much longer hug. She's holding back tears as she opens the car door and slides behind the wheel.

Juan, knowing Maria is starting to feel left out said, "Maria, I feel funny asking this because you don't know me very well. But, I'm staying here at the Mission Ranch tonight in a place they call the Bunkhouse, and it has two bedrooms. I don't want you to get the wrong idea, but it's late and you're welcome to stay if you can or if you want to."

Again Maria looks to Emma for support, where she gets a smile and a nod. Maria wipes her eyes, smiles, "Thank you Juan, that sounds so nice, but I don't want to impose on you."

"I'd like you to stay. It's a bunkhouse, not the Honeymoon Cottage like some people around here have rented."

Juan and Maria look over at Emma and Charlie, who are trying, but not successfully, for an innocent look. And they both break into smiles and shrug.

Maria smiled and nodded, "You know, it sounds good and I've had more to drink than I ever have."

As they enter the Bunkhouse, Maria said, "Oh, my gosh, this place is gorgeous and so big."

Juan said, "You take the large bedroom."

She felt like saying, "There's no reason to mess up two beds." But settled on, "Are you sure?"

He smiles and nods." Yes."

She gives him a long tight hug, their faces press together, and she whispers, "Okay. I guess I'll see you in the morning. I had a really nice time tonight, Juan."

Juan said, "Me too. It was a very special evening."

After a shower, Juan slips into bed. As he's laying there, he hears the shower running in the other room for about five minutes and then it was quiet. He wonders if he should have maybe made a move to sleep with her, but he liked her too much to be pushy, and it just wasn't his nature. As he started to dose off, he heard a light tap on the door and then it slowly opened.

"Juan, are you asleep?"

"No, I'm not."

Maria came in and sat down on the side of his bed and said, "Juan, this evening has been so overwhelming. And I mean in a good way. You and Charlie and Emma and the money. I don't know, it's like a dream. But I'm afraid, because dreams aren't reality. They don't last. If I'd gotten into my car and headed home tonight, even though I'd have the money, I would have been really sad. And now, with you, I'm just extending a dream, that won't last." She gets tears in her eyes and continues, "I was in bed in the other room and part of me wished this evening had never happened. She shook her head, "I'm so sorry, I shouldn't say things like that."

Juan sits up and puts his arm around her, "Maria, I understand what you're saying. You're tired and overwhelmed. Why don't you lay down here for while. I don't think you should be by yourself tonight. You can use my shirt over there for a nightgown."

She nods and smiles, "Okay."

Juan, jokingly, "You don't snore, do you?"

She manages a smile and laughs, "I don't think so."

"Well, okay, climb in."

As she crawled into bed she said, "This not something that I've done before. I mean, you know, but I just feel comfortable with you."

He nodded, "I'm glad."

"I've never really gotten on with my life after my husband was gone. I guess I just thought that he might show up some day, but deep down I knew he wouldn't."

Maria is laying on her back. Juan's head is resting on his elbow as he listens. "They never did find him. And missing in action sure doesn't mean that he died. Well, according to the government anyway. And I guess I've mistakenly trusted the government too long or something."

Juan, now with tears in his eyes, gently moves his head next to hers. She feels his tears running down his cheek, "Oh, no, now I've turned the perfect evening into something sad."

Juan whispered, "No, you've turned this into something real. I'm glad you feel comfortable talking about this with me. It's just disturbing that you've had to go through so much pain for so long."

He kissed her lips gently, "Maria, I'm not a good bachelor. I don't go around looking for women. I tend to think that destiny plays a part in people that we meet. And it seems like, well things just fall into place when left on their own accord. But I do like being with you."

"Juan, would you mind just holding me for the night?"

"No, I don't mind at all. It's been a long day. But you know, just being with you today and right now, made it a perfect way to end a wonderful day."

She snuggles against him, sighs and quietly said, "Oh thank you," as she closed her eyes and dropped off to sleep, with a smile on her face.

Honeymoon Cottage

The Honeymoon Cottage has a queen size sofa sleeper, a gas fireplace, and off in another area, a dinette. The place even has a private patio and yard.

Charlie said, “What a nice place.” Emma smiles and nods as takes his hand as they enter the bedroom that has a king size bed and a bath area off to the side.

Emma said, “Look at the size of that bed.”

Charlie said, “I feel guilty about you paying for all of this. It just doesn’t seem right.”

Emma unbuttoned her long black skirt and placed it in a chair, takes off her nylons and then her white blouse, turns her back to Charlie and lets him unhook her bra which she throws into a chair. Now in her panties only, which are clinging to her shapely bottom, she faces the bed, slides her panties down one leg and then the other, steps out of them, turns her head toward Charlie with a her eyebrows raised and a seductive smile.

Charlie smiles, “It’s starting to seem a little more right. A person has to know where to the draw the line on principles.”

Emma smiles and nods, “Thought you might see it my way you tree trimming hunk.” Charlie just shakes his head and smiles.

Bunkhouse Morning

Juan was awake staring at the ceiling when Maria woke. She rested her elbow on the pillow and propped her head up on her hand as she looked at him.

He rolled onto his side, faced her and said, "Hi."

She had a somber expression as she whispered, "I'm sorry I was so depressing last night. I was tired and overwhelmed, but I had no right act to that way. It wasn't fair to you."

He shook his head, "Maria, don't be sorry. I understood what you were talking about. You've been through a lot and getting too many things too quickly can be like over eating. I'm sure it brought to mind your husband, and I know money can never replace him."

She smiled, there was something about Juan's genuine sincerity that triggered a sensual sensation that enticed her to move her body tightly against him. She then put her face against his and said, "Thank you."

Their lips came together and she could feel him respond, intensifying the sensation. She slipped out of her panties and he slowly and gently rolled over on her. Both were breathing hard afterwards as they laid close together, looking in each others eyes. He smiled and said, "I guess we need to exercise more"

She smiled, sighed, and said, "Yes, it was quite a workout. But one I could get used to."

He nodded and kissed her.

Breakfast at Mission Ranch

As they sat drinking coffee and waiting for their breakfast Maria said, "What exactly do you and Charlie do, Juan?"

"I'm Emma and Charlie's gardener."

Maria's thinking they must pay gardeners quite well in San Diego, when Emma added, "Well, that's partly true, but he's the gardener for several hundred people." Maria looks puzzled.

Emma continued, "How many contracts do you have Juan?"

He shrugged, "I'm not sure."

Maria nods, "Oh, so you have a landscape company." Juan nods and then Maria looks at Charlie, "How about you Charlie?"

Charlie said, "Well, I'm a technical writer but I'm out of work. But I do write fiction when I don't have a real job."

"So, you're a writer."

Charlie, looking quite insightful said, "You know, I worked with a guy who pretty much summed it when he said, "you can write for years and not be considered a writer. But, if you steal one thing, you become a thief." That brought a few chuckles and smiles.

Juan said, "If anybody is interested in seeing the Big Sur Area from the air, the plane seats four?"

Both Emma and Maria look very surprised. Finally Maria said, "A plane? My goodness, Juan, you must really cut a nice grass to be able to afford a plane." Juan smiles and nods and the others laugh.

Arial Panorama

As they fly above the California's Big Sur area, looking over Highway 1 snaking close to the edge of the cliffs, Juan says, "As you may know, Kim Novak has or had a house on a cliff in the Big Sur area and her bath area has a huge window that overlooks the ocean. Some pilots claim to have flown along the cliff where her house is and could see her bath area through the window. Some even claim to have seen her in the bathtub."

Charlie asked, "Is that part of the tour?"

Juan laughed, "No, that's an "E" ticket. We're not going there today. But if you look down below us you can see Doris Day's home. She has horses and you can see her pasture near the house."

Emma said, "Oh, and you know Henry Miller lived in Big Sur when he wrote some very steamy stuff."

Maria said, "Oh yes, Tropic of Cancer. Of course, I've never read any of it."

Emma said, "Oh no, me either." They all laughed.

Emma continued, "Maria, why don't you come to San Diego and visit us sometime. You could stay at my place or maybe Juan has a spare room."

"That sounds nice, but it's a long drive. And I don't know if I could handle the Los Angeles traffic."

Juan interrupted, "I'll fly down and pick you up. Just let me know when you want to come."

"Really, you'd pick me up?"

"Of course."

As they fly along looking down at the scenery and houses along the cliffs, suddenly, a very small plane appears, seemingly out of nowhere, and flying fairly close to the cliff in the vicinity of where Kim Novak's house is.

Charlie points and says, "He must have gotten the "E" ticket, huh."

Juan smiles, nods and says, "It seems like it would be something John Denver would have done. You know he crashed his plane in Monterey Bay"

Maria nods and said, "Oh yes, what a terrible thing, such a tragedy." And then she starts singing:

"All my bags are packed, I'm ready to go.

I'm standing here outside your door.

I hate to wake you up to say good-bye.

But the dawn is breaking, it's early morn, the taxi's waiting He's blowing his horn.

Already I'm so lonesome I could die.

So kiss me and smile for me.

Tell me that you'll wait for me, hold me like you'll never let me go.

'Cause I'm leaving on a jet plane, don't know when I'll be back again.

Oh, babe, I hate to go".

Emma smiled, "Maria, what a beautiful voice."

Maria smiled, "Oh, thanks. I just love his music." Then she said, "You know Juan, I was wondering about something."

"What's that?"

"Well, is there chance you could spend an extra day or two here, maybe stay with me? I have one of his albums we could listen to."

Juan smiled, "Yeah, I can work that out."

Emma, with a devious smile, "Oh yeah, I'm sure you're going to be listening to a lot of albums."

Maria smiling, "Well, we might get through a couple of them. And, I'll bet Juan can whip out a tune and we could get a duet going."

Charlie couldn't hold back as he said, "Yeah, I'm sure Juan could whip out something." They laughed.

Emma said, "Well, next time we see you two, you'd better have a pretty good talent show ready."

Maria looks over at Juan, puts her hand on his thigh, raises her eyebrows while smiling, and said, "Be careful what you ask for. I didn't say the duet would necessarily be singing."

The End

About the Author:

Glen Watson was born in Glasgow, Montana, lived in Saco, Montana and moved to Salinas, California as teenager. He spent many hours scuba diving in Monterey Bay at Monastery Beach. He later joined the U.S. Navy, where he became a submariner, serving aboard diesel and nuclear fast attack submarines. He now lives in Fairhope, Alabama with his wife Marg, and 2 dogs, Sadie and Jerry.

His first novel was: Monterey Bay 1960: Lady of Cannery Row – a romantic adventure and coming of age tale with 19-year old scuba diver Robert, who discovers the joys of the underwater beauty of Monterey Bay and a passionate encounter with a lady on Cannery Row.

He recently wrote, Riker's Lot, the story of a young boy that tells his abrasive beer drinking little league coach to go to hell. And Dolphins for Sara, a story of woman navy officer that volunteers to go aboard a fast attack nuclear submarine for sixty days to determine changes that would have to be made for women on fast attack submarines.

32106546R00069

Made in the USA
San Bernardino, CA
28 March 2016